"I suspect you're every man's dream mistress, Rosemary. No strings, no commitment, no future planned. Just the promise of sex whenever we want it, wherever we want it." His voice deepened. "However we want it."

"Oh, there's going to be some sort of commitment," she told him, hoping she sounded as confident as her words. She needed to get something straight, although her heart constricted when she said, "Until we call a halt I'll be faithful to you, and I'll expect the same from you."

The dark head bent in an autocratic nod. "Very well, then. It's a deal."

The words were blunt—as blunt as hers had been.

"It's a deal," she whispered, and held out her hand.

His mouth was a thin line, strangely ruthless, as they shook hands. But it gentled when he lifted her hand to his mouth and kissed her fingertips.

The sensuous caress sent more wanton excitement tingling through Rosie. And then he bent his head and kissed her again, and his mouth took her into that realm where thought and logic no longer mattered, where the only reality was Gerd's passion and her abandoned response.

But even as she yielded she wondered how he might react if he realized she'd never done this before.

ROBYN DONALD

Greetings! I'm often asked what made me decide to be a writer of romances. Well, it wasn't so much a decision as an inevitable conclusion. Growing up in a family of readers helped; after anxious calls from neighbors driving our dusty country road, my mother tried to persuade me to wait until I got home before I started reading the current library book, but the lure of those pages was always too strong.

Shortly after I started school I started whispering stories in the dark to my two sisters. Although most of those tales bore a remarkable resemblance to whatever book I was immersed in, there were times when a new idea would pop into my brain—my first experience of the joy of creativity.

Growing up in New Zealand, in the subtropical north, gave me a taste for romantic landscapes and exotic gardens. But it wasn't until I was in my mid-twenties that I read a Harlequin romance and realized that the country I love came alive when populated by strong, tough men and spirited women.

By then I was married and a working mother, but into my busy life I crammed hours of writing; my family has always been hugely supportive, even the various dogs who have slept on my feet and demanded that I take them for walks at inconvenient times. I learned my craft in those busy years, and when I finally plucked up enough courage to send off a manuscript, it was accepted. The only thing I can compare that excitement to is the delight of bearing a child.

Since then it's been a roller-coaster ride of fun and hard work and wonderful letters from fans. I see my readers as intelligent women who insist on accurate backgrounds as well as an intriguing love story, so I spend time researching as well as writing.

THE DISGRACED PRINCESS

ROBYN DONALD

~ THE WEIGHT OF THE CROWN ~

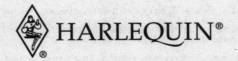

TORONTO • NEW YORK • LONDON
AMSTERDAM • PARIS • SYDNEY • HAMBURG
STOCKHOLM • ATHENS • TOKYO • MILAN • MADRID
PRAGUE • WARSAW • BUDAPEST • AUCKLAND

Recycling programs
for this product may
not exist in your area.

ISBN-13: 978-0-373-52802-8

THE DISGRACED PRINCESS

Previously published in the U.K. under the title
THE VIRGIN AND HIS MAJESTY

First North American Publication 2011

Copyright © 2009 by Robyn Donald

THE DISGRACED
PRINCESS

CHAPTER ONE

As CORONATION balls went, Rosie Matthews thought, surveying the palace ballroom, this one in Carathia had to be about as good as it got.

Wherever she looked flowers glowed richly against the white and gold walls. Men in the austere black and white of formal evening clothes radiated power and privilege, and beautiful women dazzled in couture so *haute* the ballroom looked like a catwalk for society's most favoured designers. Light from the gilded ballroom chandeliers scintillated opulently from famous and priceless tiaras, earrings and necklaces.

And every other woman in the ballroom seemed tall and impossibly elegant, including the one beside her. Hani Crysander-Gillan, Duchess of Vamili and sister-in-law of the newly crowned Grand Duke Gerd, was another racehorse, and the tiara glittering against her dark hair featured the rare and beautiful fire diamonds from her homeland of Moraze.

'I envy you,' Rosie told her cheerfully. 'This will be the only coronation ball I'll ever attend, but to get a good view I really need to stand on one of those gilded chairs. Still, I've never seen so many fabulous jewels. And the clothes—wow!' She gave an elaborate sigh. 'I feel like the proverbial poor relation. And I'm not even a relation!'

Hani laughed. 'A likely story. You look stunning, and you know it. I don't know how you managed to find something the exact honey-amber of your hair.'

Rosie glanced down at her balldress. 'It was a stroke of luck; there's a really good vintage shop just around the corner from my flat. And this doesn't seem to have been worn much. It doesn't look ten years old.'

'Who cares how old it is? It's a classic.'

Certainly its body-skimming flow gave Rosie some much-needed extra height, assisted by a pair of killer heels that had cost her almost the last of her savings.

Hani raised her brows. 'It's not like you to be afflicted with self-doubt. What's the matter?'

'It's not self-doubt, it's the realisation that the jewellery alone must be worth more than most small countries,' Rosie returned airily.

She lied. Prince Gerd Crysander-Gillan, Grand Duke and ruler of Carathia—crowned only that day—happened to be dancing right in front of her with the woman expected to become his bride. Princess Serina was yet another willowy, impossibly beautiful creature, her dark hair sleeked into an elegant chignon that showed off the diamonds of her family tiara to perfection.

'And the fact that every other woman in this room is at least ten centimetres taller than I am and wearing a tiara,' Rosie went on mournfully, before flashing Hani a gamine grin. 'However, being short means no one can see me, and Gerd won't expect glitz from a cousin by marriage.'

Especially a cousin by marriage who'd just finished

her degree, only to discover that the job market had dried up.

Lifting her small, round chin, she let her eyes roam across the dancers. Inevitably they found the man who'd invited her—and hundreds of others—to his rich little country to celebrate his coronation. As Rosie's gaze found his arrogantly handsome face Gerd smiled at the princess in his arms, then lifted his black head and looked across the ballroom, his boldly chiselled features radiating force and authority.

Flushing, Rosie lowered her eyes. Of course he wasn't looking at—far less *for*—her. He was just making sure everything was going according to plan. Gerd always had a plan, as well as the ruthless determination to carry it through, no matter what the obstacles.

A hungry longing ached through her. She'd been so certain the tenuous thread of hope that had kept her dangling for years would be severed once she saw him with the glamorous, entirely suitable Princess Serina.

Instead, coming to Carathia, seeing him again, had reignited a fire that had never died.

So who's being melodramatic? she mocked silently. How could a fire die when it had never really been lit? OK, so three years ago—on the other side of the world—she and Gerd had been thrown together for a whole magical summer.

Although they'd known each other all her life, things had changed during those long, hot weeks, but even at eighteen Rosie had been wary. Gerd was almost twelve years older, and probably a couple of centuries further advanced in sophistication. As well, her mother's lamentable history with men had coloured Rosie's outlook, so although she'd become giddy with excitement whenever he smiled at her, she'd masked it with the brash, cheerful façade she'd made her defence against the world.

Yet while they'd sailed, swum, ridden horses and talked at length about almost everything, her childhood affection for Gerd gradually developed into a deeper emotion, something that shimmered with a promise she didn't dare recognise—until the night before he went away.

When he had kissed her...

And Rosie had gone up in flames, all fears forgotten in a shocking, mesmerising rush of passion. He'd muttered her name and tried to pull away, but she'd clung, and as if he too was caught in the grip of some elemental summons he'd kissed her again, and then again, his arms tightening around her while every kiss took her deeper and deeper into unknown, thrilling territory.

How long they'd kissed she never knew, but each sensuous exploration stoked the fire that burned away her virginal inhibitions, and she was crushed against his lean, strong body in an ecstasy of surrender when he suddenly jerked free.

And said in a thick, impeded voice, 'I must be *mad*.'

Chilled, the intoxicating hunger rapidly vanishing, she'd dragged in a painful, jarring breath, unable to speak, unable to feel anything but an icy, bitter wash of humiliation at his rejection.

He'd straightened and stepped back further. In a controlled, coldly remote voice he said, 'Rosemary, I should not have done that. Forgive me. You still have a lot of growing up to do. Enjoy university, and try not to break too many hearts.'

A small, cynically rueful smile tugged at the corners of her mouth. The only heart that had been affected was hers. For the first—and only—time in her life Rosie had known the wild, intoxicating charge of desire.

Why hadn't it happened again? She'd met men almost as handsome as Gerd, men with reputations as superb lovers, and not one had stirred her emotions, not one had summoned that ravishment of her senses, as though she'd die if it wasn't satisfied...

Only Gerd.

Her eyes narrowed slightly when Gerd said something to his partner. The princess lifted her face and smiled, and they looked so utterly *right* together that Rosie winced at a stark return of the aching emptiness that had followed Gerd's departure that summer.

Whatever had happened during those enchanted weeks—the companionship, the closeness—had meant nothing to him. Not once had he contacted Rosie. News of him came through his brother, Kelt.

Don't be an idiot, she told herself robustly. Of course he hadn't contacted her. Once he'd left New Zealand his life had been packed with action and events.

Immediately after he'd arrived in Carathia his grandmother, the Grand Duchess, named him heir to her throne, and he'd had to deal with disaffection amongst the mountain people—disorder that became riots, and had then turned into a nasty little civil war.

No sooner had it been decisively won than Princess Ilona slipped into the lingering final illness that forced

Gerd to become the de facto ruler of Carathia. A year of official mourning had followed her death.

Which had given her three years to break free of the spell of the hot, lazy days she'd spent falling in love.

It wasn't through lack of trying. She'd kissed enough would-be lovers to gain herself a reputation as a tease, but nothing—and no one—had matched the sensuous magic of Gerd's kisses. Flirting had become a defence; she used it as a glossy, sparkling shield against any sort of true intimacy.

How *pathetic* to be still a virgin!

Yet when she did make love she wanted it to mean something—and she wasn't going to succumb until her feelings matched the hungry passion Gerd had summoned so effortlessly in her.

Rosie focused her attention on the rest of the dancing throng, but inevitably her gaze crept back to Gerd and his partner.

He was looking over Princess Serina's head, straight at Rosie. For a heart-stopping second she thought she read anger in his topaz-gold survey before the woman in his arms said something, and he glanced back at her.

Rosie's heart thumped violently and a swift flare of colour burned up through her skin. Turning to Hani, she gave a quick nod in the general direction of the dance floor and forced her voice into its normal insouciant tone. 'They look good together, don't they?'

Hani was silent a moment before saying slowly, 'Yes. Yes, they do.'

Rosie would have liked very much to ask what was behind the equivocal note in her voice, but the music stopped then, and Kelt, Gerd's younger brother and

Hani's husband, came up. Hani's face broke into the smile she kept only for him.

Rosie sighed silently; even after several years of marriage and a gorgeous little son, Hani and Kelt still looked at each other like lovers. And, when the band struck up again after the interval, she watched them melt into each other's arms on the dance floor and fought back a shaming surge of envy, of wonder that they'd found such joy and satisfaction, when she...

When she'd let a memory rule her life. One summer of laughing, stimulating companionship and a few passionate kisses had fuelled a futile desire without any chance of fulfilment.

Enough's enough, she thought on a sudden spurt of defiance. She was tired of being moonstruck. From now on—from this moment, in fact—it was officially over. She'd find some nice man and discover what sex was all about, get rid of this humiliating, futile hangover from the past—

'Rosemary.'

The floor shifted under her feet and her stomach contracted as though bracing for a blow. She sucked in a sharp breath before slowly turning to look up into Gerd's face, its angular features imprinted with the intimidating heritage of a thousand years of rule.

Here it was again, that seductive, treacherous ache of longing, almost more potent than the physical hunger that accompanied it. Pride persuaded her to ignore the shivers tingling down her spine.

'Hello, Gerd,' she said, hoping her voice was as steady and cool as his. 'Why can I never get you or my mother to call me Rosie?'

His wide shoulders lifted fractionally. 'I don't know. That, surely, is up to you?'

Rosie's snort was involuntary. 'Try telling Eva to shorten my name and see how far you get,' she told him briskly. 'And I seem to remember asking you quite often to call me Rosie. You never did.'

'You didn't ask—you commanded,' he said with a faint smile. 'I didn't take kindly to being ordered about by a tiny snip some twelve years younger.'

You are *not* in love with him, she reminded herself with desperate insistence. You never have been.

All she had to do was get him out of her bloodstream, out of her head, and see him as a man, not the compelling, powerful, unattainable lover of her fantasies.

'Dance with me.'

Her brave determination melted under a sudden surge of heat. To be in his arms again...

Resisting the seductive impact of that thought, she summoned a smile glinting with challenge. 'And *you* have the audacity to accuse *me* of ordering people about?'

'Perhaps I should rephrase my request,' he said on a note that held more than a hint of irony. 'Rosemary, would you like to dance with me?'

'That's much more like it,' she said sedately, hanging on to her composure by a thread. 'Yes, of course I'll dance with you.'

His mouth quirked at her formality, and something jabbed her heart. It took a determined effort of will to walk beside him onto the dance floor.

But when Gerd took her in his arms her natural sense of rhythm almost deserted her. Concentrating fiercely, she followed his lead. In that dazzling, dazed summer they'd danced together several times and she'd never forgotten the sensation of being held against his big frame, the way she'd felt so deliciously overpowered by his size and latent strength.

Now, close to him again, every cell in her body sang a wanton song of desire.

You're not in love with him, she repeated fervently. Not a bit. Never have been…

This was merely physical, a matter of hormones and hero-worship. He'd imprinted her the way a mother goose imprinted her goslings.

The thought curved her mouth in an involuntary smile. How apt. She was behaving just like a goose!

Gerd broke a silence that threatened to drag on too long. 'How long is it since we've danced together?'

'I don't know.'

That was a stupid response, an instinctive attempt at defence. And he'd noticed. Defiantly Rosie cocked her head and met his unusual eyes, tawny and arrogant as an eagle's.

Hoping her tone projected amusement tinged with nostalgia, she continued, 'Oh, yes, of course I do. How could I forget? It was my first grown-up party, do you remember? You were on holiday in New Zealand that summer.'

'I remember.' His voice was lazy, as amused as hers, the dark lashes almost hiding his eyes.

'You gave me my very first grown-up kisses,' she told him, and laughed before adding, 'Ones that set an impossibly high standard.'

If she'd thought to startle him, she failed.

'There have been plenty to judge them by since then, I understand,' he said austerely.

Disconcerted, she demanded, 'How do you know that?'

Again he shrugged, the muscles flexing beneath her fingertips. 'Information travels fast in this family of ours,' he told her laconically.

Rosie pointed out, 'Except that I'm not proper family. The only connection is that my father's first wife was your cousin. A fairly distant cousin at that. So I'm actually flying false colours. Everyone seems to think I'm a Crysander-Gillan, instead of a very ordinary Matthews!'

'Nonsense,' he said negligently, adding with an oblique smile, 'There's nothing ordinary about you. Anyway, your half-brother *is* my blood relation as well as a good friend, and Alex would very properly have told me where to go if you hadn't been invited.'

Of course she'd been aware that only Gerd's ironbound sense of duty had led to this invitation, but his laconic acknowledgement of it stung nevertheless.

Stifling her hurt, Rosie switched her gaze to the half-brother she'd never really known. Her parents' marriage had disintegrated before she was old enough to realise that the boy who appeared occasionally in her life was actually related to her.

Gerd's arm around her tightened; Alex forgotten, she followed the almost imperceptible command and matched her steps to her partner's. A sensuous thrill ran through her as they pivoted, their bodies meeting for an intimate moment.

Heat flamed through her at that subtle pressure; she

dragged in a painful breath, only to find it imbued with the potent aphrodisiac of Gerd's faint body scent—pure, charged masculinity. She was becoming aroused, readying herself for a passion that would never be returned, never be appeased.

And then Gerd drew back and she felt the distance between them like a chasm.

Determined to break the sense of connection, the feverish hunger, she said bleakly, 'You know Alex better than I do. My mother banished him to boarding school before I was born, and we rarely saw him.'

'He told me you're having difficulty finding a job.'

Startled, she lifted her head, parrying his coolly questioning survey. 'For someone on the opposite side of the world from New Zealand you certainly keep your finger on the pulse,' she said forthrightly. 'Yes, the downturn in business has meant that inexperienced commerce graduates are in over-supply, but I'll find something.'

'Surely Alex could fit you into his organisation?'

'Any position I get will be on my own merits,' she told him abruptly.

'I'm flattered you allowed him to pay your way here. He said he had to almost force you to accept the offer.'

Her brother had dropped in on her the day she got the invitation, and when she'd told him she couldn't afford to go, he'd lifted one black brow and drawled, 'Consider it your next Christmas present.'

She'd laughed and refused, but a few days later his secretary had rung to ask if she had a passport, and given her instructions to meet his private jet at Auckland's airport. And her mother had applied pressure, no doubt hoping that a holiday among the rich and famous would make Rosie reconsider her next move—to find a job in a florist's shop.

'You might just as well be a hairdresser,' Eva Matthews had wailed. 'It was bad enough when you decided to take a commerce degree, but to turn yourself into a *florist*?' She'd startled Rosie with her virulence. 'Why, for heaven's sake? Everyone says you're clever as a cartload of monkeys, but you've done nothing—nothing at all!—with your brains. You were a constant disappointment to your father—what would he have thought of this latest hare-brained scheme?'

Rosie had shrugged. Starting with the fact that she'd been born the wrong sex, she'd never been able to please her parents.

'This is something *I* want to do,' she said firmly.

Her years at an expensive, exclusive boarding school had been for her mother. University had been for her father, although he'd made his disapproval clear when she'd chosen a commerce degree instead of something more academically challenging that would befit the daughter of a famed archaeologist.

Neither of her parents had known that she'd always planned to work with flowers. The degree had been her first step, and during her holidays she'd worked in a good florist's shop, honing her skills and a natural talent for design. A few months before the end of the university year the shop had closed down, a casualty of the recession, and, with the financial world on the brink of panic, now was not the time to set up. Even if she'd had the capital, which she didn't.

Rosie had discussed her situation with Kelt. He'd advised finding a job, saving like crazy and waiting for an upturn in the situation.

Good advice. Her expression unconsciously wistful, she turned her head and watched him dance with Hani. They looked so perfect together...

Just as Gerd and the Princess Serina had looked—a matching pair.

'They are very happy together,' Gerd said, an abrasive note in his words startling her.

'Oh, yes, so happy. But who wouldn't be, married to Kelt?'

Kelt didn't write her off as a lightweight or treat her as though she had the common sense of a meringue. A growing girl couldn't have had a better substitute brother, but his marriage to Hani had taken something from the special relationship he and Rosie shared; he had other loyalties, other responsibilities now.

Rosie had expected it to happen and she didn't resent it, but she missed their closeness.

Gerd asked laconically, 'So what is your plan?'

'Oh, take a look around, see what I can find,' she said airily. 'And what are your plans, now that you and the country have emerged from the year of mourning? What changes are you going to make in Carathia?'

'Only a few, and those slowly. I didn't realise you were interested in my country.'

She met his eyes with a swift, dazzling smile. 'Of course I am. Being related to the ruler of Carathia gave me immense prestige at school. I used to boast about it incessantly.'

He held her away from him, examining her face. Bracing herself as a flame of awareness sizzled through her, Rosie met that intent eagle-amber gaze with cool challenge.

The grimness faded from his expression, although his smile was narrow as a blade. 'I don't believe that for a moment. Why did you decide to become an accountant?'

She wasn't going to tell him about her love affair with flowers. 'It just seemed a sensible thing to do. As I'm sure you're aware, my father was hopeless with money—he spent everything on his expeditions—and my mother isn't much better. I wanted to know how things worked in the financial world.'

Cynicism tinged his deep voice. 'Or did you just decide to shock your parents?'

She shook her head, stopping abruptly when her curls bobbed about in a childish fashion. 'I wanted to come away from university with something concrete, skills I could use.'

Something that made people see past her outward physical attributes. Most people took one look at her and wrote her off as a flirtatious little piece of fluff.

On a cool note she finished, 'And I don't regret it at all.'

Gerd looked sceptical. The music swelled, and he caught her closer to steer her around a slight traffic jam of dancers ahead. Resisting the quick, fierce temptation to let herself relax against him, Rosie followed his steps.

Above her head he said, 'You asked what changes I plan; in parts of Carathia change is treated with suspicion, so I'll be treading carefully, but I intend to extend the scope and the range of education, especially in the mountain districts.'

'Why education? What about health?'

Broad shoulders lifted in another swift shrug. 'My grandmother concentrated on health services. They're well-established, but not as fully used as they could be, especially in the mountains where superstition is still rampant and many people prefer to use the local wise women. When patients do finally present at hospitals, they often die there.'

Rosie nodded. 'So I suppose they try even harder not to go near them.'

'Exactly.'

'And you think education will help? How?'

'By giving children an understanding of science and some knowledge of the outer world. Life in the mountains is still very insular, very remote. Children in the alpine villages have to travel to the bigger towns for secondary education, so most miss out. I want to take higher education—*good* higher education—to each market town.'

'It seems logical,' she said thoughtfully. 'What's the school leaving age?'

'Thirteen. Far too young, but parents say they need them at home to help with farming, so any alteration will have to be managed with tact.'

Gerd felt her curls tickle his throat when she nodded.

Thoughtfully she said, 'To change attitudes you need to corral them at school while they're still open and receptive. How are you going to set up this system of a high school in every valley?' She glanced up at him, wide blue eyes intent and serious for once. 'I assume that's what you're planning?'

Gerd told her, sardonically amused because he was discussing his plans for Carathia with the precocious, light-hearted girl-child who'd jolted him with the passion in her kisses—and his own violent and unconsidered response to them.

That summer three years ago had revealed that behind her sexy, laughing face lurked a keen, quick brain. He'd enjoyed their discussions, but her ardent kisses on the final night when he'd yielded to the forbidden temptation of her sultry mouth had reminded him she was far too young and innocent to do what he'd wanted to do—carry her off to the nearest bed and make reckless, sensuous love to her.

Thank God he'd rejected her open invitation. Etched into his brain was the sight of her kissing Kelt the very morning after she'd turned to flames in his arms. He'd realised then that she'd been using him as a substitute for the man she really wanted.

Did she still long for his brother? If her expression when she watched Kelt dancing with Hani was anything to go by, it seemed more than likely.

Kelt had always been there for her when her father was away searching for ancient civilisations, when her mother was off with the latest boyfriend. A beautiful woman with everything going for her, Eva Matthews wasted her life chasing some sort of rainbow fantasy of the perfect love. Judging by the stream of men through her university years, her daughter was doing the same.

Searching for a security she'd never known? Possibly. Trouble in a delicious little package?

Undoubtedly. But she was no longer naïve and inexperienced.

Above her froth of amber curls he sketched a humourless smile. He was acutely aware of her small, elegantly curved form in that sinuous dress, its colour reminding him of the beaches on his brother's estate in New Zealand. Subtly glittering, the fabric made the most of her curves and narrow waist without clinging. In a room full of women clothed to impress, she stood out because she wore no jewellery at all, not even a ring on a slender finger.

A strand of hair snagged itself on his lapel, glittering in the light of the chandeliers. She jerked free and said, 'Sorry about that. I did try for dignity, but my curls are uncontrollable.'

'It would seem so.' His voice sounded odd in his ears, and he frowned, fighting back a swift, elemental appetite, a headstrong physical goad that knotted his gut and dried his mouth.

Half smiling, she gazed up at him, dark lashes wide around the intense, gold-flecked blue of her eyes. 'I straightened my hair once and it just hated it and went all lank and limp, so now I let the curls do their own thing.'

Gerd closed his mind against a swift, erotic image of her, sleek and golden and laughing against crisp white sheets, but the maddening questions refused to go away. Would she be as passionate as the promise of her soft, laughing mouth?

Hard on the heels of that came another question, even more insubordinate. Was she like this—provocative, tempting—with her lovers?

Of course she was. And now she was twenty-one and experienced, there was no need for restraint...

CHAPTER TWO

GERD dampened down a compelling surge of desire to say remotely, 'Although you affect to despise your hair, it's very pretty. As I'm sure you know.'

Rosie should have been gratified; apart from that final crack about her hair—delivered with aloof kindness, as though she were ten—he had at least treated her like an adult.

Unfortunately, since they'd moved onto the floor she'd reacquired a taste for the danger and zest of crossing swords with Gerd. Like fencing with a tiger, she'd decided dreamily three years ago.

Her pulse rate skyrocketed when her glance skimmed the strong, boldly chiselled features, intimidating yet profoundly sexy. Now she understood why she'd always been attracted to men with a slight cleft in their chin and hawkish profiles.

Rapidly discarding her first impetuous response, she told him briskly, 'I could say, just *you* try living with a head covered with red curls and see if anyone takes you seriously, but instead I'll ignore your remark. I'll bet you were born looking like a king.'

His smile was lazy, almost teasing. 'I'm not a king, and it was meant to be a compliment.'

'Then I'm afraid you'll have to try harder.'

His eyes narrowed, and for a second—perhaps less?—something flashed between them, a brittle tension that robbed her of words and breath.

To her relief the music died away, and he released her and offered his arm. She rested her hand on it, feeling insignificant as he escorted her to where Kelt, Hani and Alex waited for her.

They were almost there when he said formally, 'Thank you for coming, Rosemary.'

'I wouldn't have missed it for the world,' she returned, smiling pleasantly at a dowager wearing a serious dress in satin and more pearls than was decent. Taking refuge in flippancy from the aching emptiness that threatened her, Rosie decided the only thing missing was a lorgnette.

She went on, 'It's been a truly amazing week. And the coronation ceremony was…' She searched for the right words, finally settling on, 'Truly awe-inspiring. Hugely impressive.' And profoundly moving.

'I'm glad you found it so,' he said, his neutral tone revealing nothing. 'You're leaving the day after tomorrow, aren't you?'

'Yes.' She'd like to ask him what he'd planned for tomorrow night, but no doubt he had better things to do than entertain a nobody from New Zealand.

Kiss Princess Serina, perhaps?

When they reached the others they talked pleasantries for a few minutes until Gerd walked away, and at last Rosie could draw breath.

All she wanted to do was skulk up to her bedroom and hide there until she felt more…well, more *herself.*

But it was almost over. If she organised her life with care and some cunning she need never exchange words or glances with Gerd again. And when the wedding invitation arrived she'd produce a very good excuse for not attending—a broken leg should do.

Even if she had to break it herself.

From the corner of her eye she saw Gerd talking to the princess, and stiffened her spine. OK, so exorcising this unwanted hunger would take willpower and a rigorous refusal to indulge in daydreams, but she could manage that—she'd had a lot of practice.

The evening wore on. Resolutely keeping her gaze away from the person who held her attention, Rosie danced and laughed and talked and flirted with several interested men. By midnight her rigid self-control was beginning to take its toll and she allowed herself another longing thought of the bed waiting for her in the private apartments of the palace.

But when the ball ended, Alex told her casually, 'Gerd's asked us to his quarters for a nightcap. Just the family.'

No princess? Rosie banished a treacherous needle of excitement. 'How kind of him.'

He lifted a brow and after an uncertain look at his handsome face she began to chatter. She loved her brother, but they had never known each other well enough to develop the sort of relationship that made for confidences.

It was definitely a family gathering—although Gerd seemed to be related to a lot of European royalty.

But no Princess Serina. Stifling an ignoble relief, Rosie refused a glass of champagne and accepted one of mineral water, then glanced around. The private drawing room was big, furnished with more than a salute to Victorian taste. It wasn't all heavy furniture, however. Her gaze travelled to the large painting in a place of honour on one wall.

'Kelt's and my New Zealand grandfather,' Gerd said from behind her. 'Alex's great-great-uncle.'

'He's very handsome,' she said inanely. 'More like Kelt than you.'

'You're intimating that I'm not handsome?' he drawled lazily.

Colour burned along her cheekbones. Keeping her eyes on the portrait, she returned in her most limpid tone, 'I'm forever being told that it's only women who need constant reassurance about their attractiveness.'

His low laugh held a sardonic note. 'Well avoided.'

'All I meant was that your grandfather and Kelt have that northern-European look, whereas you show your Mediterranean heritage.' And a drop-dead gorgeous set of genes he'd inherited—a strong-boned face emphasised by those raptor's eyes and his powerful, long-legged physique.

'Like most ruling families, the Crysander-Gillans have a very mixed heritage. The original founder of my house was a Norseman who arrived here with a group of Vikings via Russia some time in the tenth century. They stayed, and imported princesses from almost every country in Europe and the occasional one from considerably further away.'

Well, Princess Serina wouldn't have far to come! Her family lived in exile on the French Riviera. Rosie's heart contracted. 'I like this portrait,' she said swiftly. 'He looks…utterly dependable, yet dangerous.'

Gerd smiled and said something in a language Rosie recognised as being Carathian. 'That's an old Carathian proverb—*A man should be a tiger in bed, a lion in battle, and wise and cunning as a fox in counsel.* The Carathians believe that my grandfather met that standard.'

Rosie kept her attention religiously fixed on the painted face. 'He looks all that and more. How did the ancient Carathians know about tigers and lions?'

He drawled, 'There used to be lions in southern Europe, and people from the Mediterranean got around— remember, Alexander the Great marched as far as India. I imagine those who made it back arrived home with stories about tigers.'

'Was Carathia part of Greece originally?'

'No, although as a state it began with a band of Greek soldiers who lost a battle a thousand years or so before the Christian era and fled this way. They found this valley, and helped the local tribespeople against an attacking force sent to control the pass. For their endeavours they were rewarded with Carathian brides.'

'I hope the brides approved,' Rosie observed tartly.

'Who knows?' He sounded amused.

Rosie's heart did a ridiculous flip. If those ancient Greeks had been anything like Gerd their brides had probably been delirious with excitement.

Gerd went on, 'Over the years various of my ancestors acquired the coastal region and its offshore islands.'

'How?' she asked, intrigued by the long history of the small country.

'Usually by conquest, sometimes by marriage.'

She asked curiously, 'How many languages do you speak?'

'Kelt and I grew up speaking both English and Carathian as first languages. We've learned a couple more along the way.'

'I'm very impressed by the way people here switch from language to language without any effort. It makes me feel very much like a country cousin.'

'Languages can be learnt. Besides, you know the one everyone understands.'

Startled, she swivelled her head to survey his face.

His eyes were half-closed, his chiselled mouth curved in a smile that hit Rosie like a charge of electricity. 'Your smile speaks the most fundamental language—that of the heart.'

'Thank you for such a pretty compliment,' Rosie said hastily, furious because her hot cheeks revealed her astonishment. 'I don't think it's true, but I'd love it to be.'

Brows raised, Gerd said, 'You're embarrassed. Why? I can't believe no other man has told you that your smile is a most potent weapon.'

More than a little wary, she said, 'Actually, no.'

Men tended to concentrate on her more physical attributes.

Relief seeped through her when a manservant came up. Gerd looked down at him and the servant said something in a low voice. After Gerd's nod the man went across to the windows and drew back the heavy drapes to reveal the starry burst of a swarm of skyrockets.

Charmed, Rosie joined in the soft murmur of appreciation around the room.

'The Carathians enjoy firework displays and have organised this,' Gerd said as the wide French windows were opened.

Everyone trooped out into the warm night onto a stone terrace. 'Come here, Rosemary,' Gerd said, making a space for her so she could see easily.

Sheer pleasure seeped through Rosie as she took her place beside him. The private apartments in the palace looked over the walls that had sheltered the people of the old town for centuries. Across the vast valley outlines of mountains reared black against a sky glittering with stars she'd never seen before.

But the stars were put to shame when more fireworks flared into life high above them, a depiction of the Carathian crown she'd watched the archbishop place on Gerd's black head earlier that day. At that moment of crowning, of Gerd's commitment to his country, a roar had risen from the crowds outside the cathedral who were watching the ceremony on big screens.

Recalling the fierce, unexpected sound echoing around the ancient stone walls, she took a deep breath. Something fragile and strange expanded within her, filling her with an almost painful anticipation.

Other displays of fireworks burst across the night sky, drowning out the stars. The royal coat of arms formed a triumphant pattern, followed by the emblem of the country—a lion rampant and then a cupped flower, pure white and beautiful.

'The national flower of Carathia,' Gerd told her. 'It blooms in the snow. To the people it symbolises the courage and strength of Carathians.'

To Rosie's horror her throat closed. Torn by an emotion

she didn't understand, she abandoned her usual flippant response. 'I suppose in the past they've often needed that symbolism.'

'Indeed they have,' Gerd said, his tone so noncommittal that Rosie looked up.

As though he sensed her regard he glanced down, his brows rising in a silent question when their eyes met. She suppressed a shiver and transferred her gaze to the flower, fading swiftly against the depthless darkness of the sky.

'You're cold,' he said quietly.

'No, not a bit.' She flashed him a swift smile. 'Just impressed all over again. This is an amazing place.'

'I'm glad you're enjoying it.'

Conventional words, meaning nothing. No fuel for dreams there, she told herself firmly, and pinned her attention to the display as once more the sky exploded into colour, this time a joyous, fiery free-for-all that eventually sank into darkness. A collective sigh seemed to whisper over the city, and in the silence someone not too far away started to play what sounded like a cornet or trumpet. The silvery, plaintive notes were unbearably moving in the quiet air.

'A folk tune,' Gerd said quietly, just for her. 'A song of lost love.'

To Rosie's utter horror, tears prickled at the backs of her eyes. She had to swallow to be able to say lightly, 'Aren't they all? The world's literature and music is built on broken hearts.'

The notes died away into a momentary silence that was followed by an eruption of cheers and the sound of horns and whistles.

Half an hour later Rosie surveyed her bedroom, decorated to pay tactful tribute to the age of the palace without sacrificing comfort, and thought of the time she'd spent in Carathia.

Watching Gerd, sophisticated and formidable amongst the world's elite, had emphasised as nothing else could the huge difference between them.

In New Zealand his heritage and position hadn't seemed so important. He'd always been dominant, that formidable inbuilt air of confidence more intimidating than arrogance could ever be. No one, least of all his New Zealand relatives, had been surprised when the business enterprise he'd set up with Kelt had turned into an empire with ramifications all over the world.

But seeing him in Carathia had added another dimension to his depth and compelling authority, giving him a mystique based on his people's affection and respect and trust.

Yes, she'd made the right—the only—decision. She wasn't going to waste her life longing for a man who could never be hers.

Shivering a little, she eased out of her dress, climbed into pyjamas and got into bed. Normally she read for a while, but nothing about the book she'd brought with her appealed, so she turned off the lamp and courted sleep.

An hour later, still wide awake, she got out of bed and padded across to her window, pulling back the drape to gaze down across the city. Although the lights had dimmed, the Carathians were still celebrating their ruler's coronation with gusto. She could hear singing, and recognised the sad beauty of the folk tune. Clearly it meant something important to the people of Carathia.

A sense of aloneness chilled her. Gerd belonged here in his palace above the city, and Kelt and Hani too, and Alex, although he possessed no royal blood, fitted easily into this gathering of the world's elite and powerful.

Rosie Matthews, unemployed, from New Zealand didn't.

Even the moon, she realised suddenly as she stared at it, was different—back to front from the one that beamed down on the other side of the world.

'So what?' she said into the night air, fragrant with scents she didn't recognise. 'Stop feeling sorry for yourself and at least get some rest.'

She must have slept for a few hours, because she dreamed—tangled images that had faded by the time she woke—but confronting her reflection the next morning made her inhale sharply and then apply cosmetics to banish the only too obvious signs of a restless night. Breakfast was served in her room, interrupted by a visit from Hani, who eyed her with concern.

Rosie pre-empted any query by saying firmly, 'I was too excited to sleep much last night—just like an overwrought kid after a birthday party.'

'Tell me about it,' Hani said in the resigned tone of a mother who'd had to deal with just that situation. 'But it was a great day, wasn't it?'

'It's been a fabulous week,' Rosie said in her airiest voice. 'Like living in the Middle Ages, only with bathrooms and electricity.'

Hani laughed, but the glance she gave Rosie was shrewd. 'You say that as though you'll be glad to get back home.'

'I will, but I'll never forget Carathia.' Or the man who now ruled it.

Hani said, 'I'd like to go straight to New Zealand, but Kelt has a meeting with the head honchos from Alex's firm in London, so we're going there first.' She gave a swift, lovely smile. 'I'll be interested to see how our little Rafi enjoys big cities.'

Hani was right—the sooner she got away from here the better, Rosie thought mordantly as she waved the family party off later that morning. Then she could stop being such an idiot.

Once back home she wouldn't spend wakeful nights wondering when Gerd was going to announce his engagement to Princess Serina.

By telling herself bracingly that it was completely stupid to feel as though her life was coming to an end, she managed to give Gerd a glittering smile when they met later that morning. In her most accusing voice, she said, 'Alex tells me you killed him while you were fencing before breakfast.'

Amused, he surveyed her. 'For a dead man he looked remarkably energetic afterwards.'

'He's disgustingly fit.' Rosie smiled, hoping it didn't look as painful as it felt. Damn it, she'd get rid of this crush no matter what it took. 'I didn't know he was a fencer.' In fact, she didn't know much about her half-brother at all.

Gerd understood, perhaps more than she liked. 'He learned at university, I believe. He's good. I believe you're using today to visit the museum.'

Rosie nodded. 'I'm looking forward to that, and afterwards I'm checking out the shopping area.'

'Just make sure you don't lose your guide—the central part of the city is like a rabbit warren and not many of the people speak English. If you got lost I'd probably have to mount a search party.'

His smile made Rosie's foolish heart flip in her chest. He isn't being *personal*, she told herself sternly.

He went on, 'I'd like to show you around myself, but my day is taken up. I'm meeting my First Minister and then farewelling guests.'

Including Princess Serina? Rosie concealed the humiliating question with her friendliest smile, the one that usually caused Kelt to view her with intense suspicion. 'Rather you than me,' she said cheerfully. 'I'm going to have a lovely day.'

She did, discovering that Carathia's national flower was actually a buttercup. New Zealand too had a mountain buttercup, and, strangely enough, it too was pristinely white.

How foolish to feel that the coincidence formed some sort of link between the two countries!

The shopping area displayed interesting boutiques and the usual big names; her guide, a pleasant woman in her thirties with an encyclopaedic knowledge of Carathia, did her best to encourage her to buy, but Rosie resisted, even the silk scarf exquisitely embroidered 'by hand', the shopkeeper told her, pointing out the fineness of the stitches. She held it up. 'And it suits you; you have the same delicate colouring, the soft clarity of spring.'

'It's lovely,' Rosie said on a sigh, 'and worth every penny, but I don't have those pennies, I'm afraid. Thank you for showing it to me, though.'

Her regret must have shown in her tone because the

woman smiled and nodded and packed the beautiful, fragile thing away without demur.

Back at the palace she found a note waiting for her. Apart from his signature on birthday and Christmas cards it was the first time she'd seen Gerd's writing; bold and full of character, it made her heart thump unnecessarily fast as she scanned the paper.

He hoped she'd had a good day, and suggested that they have dinner together at a restaurant he knew, one where they wouldn't be hounded by photographers.

And where they wouldn't be alone, she thought with a wry quirk of her lips. Perhaps the princess objected to him dining with another woman in the privacy of his palace apartment, even when the other woman was related by marriage.

It was probably only his excellent manners that stopped him pleading a previous appointment and avoiding her altogether.

Temptation warred viciously with common sense. Should she go or do the sensible thing and say she was too tired? In the end her weaker part won. What harm could a dinner with him do, chaperoned as they'd be by the other diners, not to mention the waiters?

She rang the bell and gave the servant her answer.

Now, what to wear?

Anticipation built rapidly inside her; just for tonight—just this once—she'd let herself enjoy Gerd's company.

After all, there weren't going to be any repercussions. She was adult enough to deal with the situation. She'd forget her foolish crush and treat him like...oh, like the other men she'd gone out with. She'd be friendly, interested, sparkle for him, even flirt a little. It would be perfectly safe because Gerd was going to marry either Princess Serina, or someone very like her.

Someone *suitable*.

And when tonight was over Rosie would never see him again. Well, not in the flesh, she thought mordantly. He had a habit of turning up in the media—arrogantly handsome royalty was always good for a headline, especially when it came to love and marriage.

Eventually she chose a slender dress in a clear, warm colour the blue of her eyes, one of Hani's rare couture mistakes. It had been shortened, of course, but the proportions were good. And so what if she'd worn it twice since arriving in Carathia? Princess Serina might have been dressed in a completely different outfit each time she'd appeared, but Rosie couldn't compete.

Ready to go, she critically eyed herself in the huge mirror and gave a bleak nod; the soft material skimmed her body so her curves weren't too obvious and the neckline was discreetly flattering.

She'd aimed for discretion in make-up too, but her glowing reflection made her wonder uneasily if she shouldn't apply a little more foundation just to tone things down. Not that foundation would mask the sparkle in her eyes.

She hesitated, then shrugged. Who was she fooling? She was going out with Gerd because she craved a tiny interlude of privacy, of something special.

To build more dreams on?

'No,' she said aloud, startling herself. 'To convince myself once and forever not to dream any more, because dreaming is a total, *useless* waste of my life and I'm over it. I'm free and twenty-one and unemployed, and I will put fairy tales behind me.'

CHAPTER THREE

STIFFENING her shoulders, Rosie turned away from her reflection, picked up a small blue evening bag and went out.

Her composure lasted exactly as long as it took for her to set eyes on Gerd.

The previous week should have accustomed her to his magnificence in austere, perfectly tailored black and white. Only it hadn't. A wild tumult beat through her blood and she had to stop herself from dragging in a shaken breath.

Don't you dare stutter like a besotted teenager, she commanded.

That horrible prospect gave her enough energy to steady her erratic breathing and say in a voice that almost sounded normal, 'You're an amazing family, you and Kelt and Alex. You're all gorgeous in your different ways even when you're in ordinary kit, but put you in evening clothes and you all take on a masculine glamour that should come with flashing signs to warn impressionable females. Most men look vaguely like penguins at formal occasions, but not you three. Have you ever been approached to model male cosmetics?'

'No.'

Just the one word, but she was left in no doubt about his feelings. Laughter bubbled up inside her. 'Alex has. He looked just like you did then.'

'I can imagine it,' Gerd said with a half-smile. 'If you think we men need warning signs, you should hand out sunglasses.'

Nonplussed, she stared at him. His face was unreadable, but she thought she saw a glint of amusement in his eyes, enough to give her voice an edge when she said, 'Thank you, I think. But it's not me, it's the dress—Hani gave it to me.'

His voice deepened. 'Nonsense, it's always been you. Hani calls you instant radiance.'

Shaken by both his words and their tone, she grabbed at her precarious poise. 'Radiance? I haven't noticed myself glowing in the dark, so I assume I'm safe.'

His eyes narrowed a fraction. 'Ah, yes, but what about those close to you?'

'I don't think you need worry,' she said kindly. 'Hani and Kelt let me play with their precious infant, and that's as good a safety recommendation as you can get.'

To her disappointment he glanced at his watch. 'We'd better go. One of the minor irritations of life here is that it's ruled by the clock.'

'Even when you're off-duty?' she asked on the way down.

'Basically I'm never off-duty.'

A car waited discreetly by one of the side doors of the palace. Two men sat in front—one in uniform, one without.

Gerd stood aside to let her in first and, once settled,

she said thoughtfully, 'I doubt if I could cope with that.'

'I've always known I was going to have to do it.' He clicked his seat belt in and glanced across at her already fastened one. 'When I was younger I was resentful of paparazzi, but I grew out of that.'

A grim note in the deep voice made her wonder how hard it had been for him to achieve that resignation. Something about the man sitting in front of her caught her eye. 'Gerd, the man in the passenger seat isn't wearing a seat belt.'

Straight brows drawing together, he told her, 'He's a bodyguard.'

'Oh.' Feeling foolish and slightly uneasy, she asked, 'Bodyguards don't?'

'No. They need to be able to react instantly.'

Perturbed at the thought of him in danger, she said, 'I didn't realise you'd need them here.'

Although she should have. Only a couple of years ago the Carathians had been fighting each other over his accession.

Quickly she asked, 'Is everything all right here now?'

He said in a tone that dismissed her concern, 'Yes, of course.'

But something his First Minister had said to him that morning echoed in Gerd's mind. 'Things are quiet now; the discovery that the ringleaders were in the pay of MegaCorp and that the purpose of the insurrection was to take over the carathite mines horrified every Carathian. And while the people are basking in the afterglow of the coronation and the harvest is on the way, no one is going to have time to call on ancient legends to back up any lingering dissatisfaction.'

Gerd trusted his judgement; the First Minister came from the mountains, where the legend that had bedevilled his ancestors for centuries had its strongest adherents.

Before Gerd could speak the older man had added, 'But with respect, sir, you need a wife. Further celebrations—a formal betrothal followed by a wedding and the birth of an heir as soon as possible—would almost certainly put an end to any plotting. Your plans for higher education should mean that the old legend will never have the hold over future generations that it has in the past.'

Gerd said grimly, 'At least we don't have to worry about further problems from MegaCorp.'

He'd seen to that, using his power in the financial world to clinically and without mercy ruin the men who'd so cynically played with other men's lives.

He glanced down at the woman beside him, lovely and eminently desirable, her wide blue eyes anxiously uplifted. Concern was in them and something else, something that disappeared so quickly he barely recognised it.

Deep inside him a fierce instinct stirred. She was so young, but it wasn't hero worship he'd caught in her gold-sprinkled eyes. If she *was* still longing for Kelt, it was a total waste of a life.

And he suspected he could do something about it…

Rosie could gather nothing from his impassive, gorgeous face. Repressing a quiver deep in the pit of her stomach, she demanded, 'What do you mean, *of course everything's all right*? I thought—'

'Once the ringleaders of the insurrection were shown to be the pawns of a foreign company who wanted to take over the mines,' he interrupted, 'the fighting stopped. No one in Carathia wanted that.'

'Of course they wouldn't.' The country's prosperity was based to a large degree on carathite, a mineral necessary in electronics. 'What happened to the people who started the rebellion?'

Gerd looked ahead. A gleam from the setting sun caught his black head, summoning a lick of blue fire. For a few seconds Rosie allowed herself to examine his profile, hungrily taking in the bold, angular outline. A potent little thrill burnt through her. His mouth should have softened his features; instead, that top lip was buttressed by a firm lower one and the cleft square of his chin.

He said calmly, 'They are no longer in any position to cause further trouble.'

This was Gerd as she'd never seen him before, his natural authority tinged with a ruthlessness that sent a chill scudding down her spine.

He turned his head, and she flushed. His brows lifted slightly, but he said in a level voice, 'Somehow I find it difficult to see you as an accountant.'

'Why?'

'As a child you adored flowers. I always assumed you'd do something with them.'

She gazed at him in astonishment. 'I'm surprised you remember.'

'I remember you being constantly scolded for picking flowers and arranging them,' he said drily.

'I grew out of that eventually. Well, I grew out of

swiping them from the nearest garden! But actually, I'm seriously thinking of setting up in business as a florist as soon as I can.'

He said thoughtfully, 'You'll need training, surely?'

Briefly she detailed the experience she had, finishing, 'I can run a shop. I have the financial knowledge, and I was left in sole charge often enough in my friend's shop to know I can do it. I helped her with weddings, formal arrangements for exclusive dinner parties, the whole works. I can make a success of it.'

'So how are you going to organise things financially?'

She kept her gaze resolutely fixed in front, but from the corner of her eye she sensed him examining her face. 'I'll manage,' she said coolly.

'Alex?'

'No.' She hesitated, then said, 'And before you ask, I'm not going to ask Kelt for backing, either.'

'I refuse to believe your mother is happy about this.'

He spoke neutrally, but she knew what he meant. 'She'll get used to it.'

He said quietly, 'You didn't have much luck with your parents, did you.' It wasn't a question. 'Your father didn't live in the modern world.'

'None of us had much luck,' she returned, forcing a note of worldliness. 'Yours died early—Alex's mother too—and mine just weren't interested in children. Still, we haven't turned out badly. Perhaps that happy home life children are supposed to need so much is just a myth.' She finished casually, 'Like perfect love.'

'Can you see Kelt and Hani together and believe either of those assumptions?'

'No,' she said instantly, ashamed of her cynicism. 'They are the real thing.'

Perhaps her envy showed in her voice because he asked rather distantly, 'Is that what you're looking for?'

'Aren't we all?' she parried, wary now. She loosened fingers that had tightened on each other in her lap, and gazed resolutely at the streetscape outside. Perfect, eternal, all-absorbing romance was the elusive chimera her mother searched for, restlessly flitting from lover to lover, but never succeeding.

Was Gerd hoping for that same eternal sense of fulfilment with Princess Serina?

She could ask him, but the words refused to come, and the moment passed as the car turned into a narrow alley in the older part of the city.

'Here we are,' he said without emphasis.

The vehicle drew up outside the heavy, ancient door of an equally ancient building. People turned to look when the security man, until then a silent presence beside the chauffeur, got out. A doorman moved across the pavement to open the car's rear door.

It was all done swiftly, discreetly, yet the smooth operation sent a chill down Rosie's spine as she and Gerd went through the door and into the building. Her own life was so free, compared to Gerd's.

On the other hand, she thought with an effort at flippancy, she wasn't rich enough to dine in places like this.

As though he could read her mind, Gerd said, 'This is the aristocratic quarter of town. In fact, right next door is the town house of the Dukes of Vamili.'

Her brow wrinkled. 'That's Kelt's title, isn't it?'

'Yes. It's used for the second son of the ruler now, but before the title was taken over by our family the Duke of Vamili was the second-ranking man in the Grand Duchy, with almost regal power over about a third of Carathia. About two hundred years ago the then Duke led a rebellion against the Grand Duke, and died for his treachery. He had only one child, a daughter, who was married off to the second son of the Grand Duke. The Grand Duke then transferred the title and all the estates—to him.'

'Poor woman,' Rosie said crisply. 'It doesn't sound like a recipe for a happy marriage.'

His smile was brief. 'Strangely enough, it appears to have been. Of course, he might have been an excellent husband. And women, especially aristocratic women, of those days didn't have such high expectations of marriage.'

'Unlike modern women, who have the audacity to want happiness and fulfilment,' Rosie returned sweetly, pacing up a wide sweep of shallow stairs.

Gerd cocked an ironic brow. 'Some seem to believe that both should come without any effort on their part.'

Like my mother, Rosie thought sombrely. Chasing rainbows all her life...

They were shown into a room that opened out through an arcade onto a stone terrace overlooking the great valley of Carathia.

Rosie sighed in involuntary appreciation, walking across to grip the stone balustrade, still warm from the sun. 'This is so beautiful, like a bowl half-filled with light.'

Dusk was creeping across the valley, and in the growing pool of shadow all that could be seen were small golden pinpoints, brave challenges to the darkness. Eastwards she could pick out groves of trees, closely planted fields of some sort of grain, clusters of red-tiled villages, the shimmer of silver-gilt that was the river and every detail on the slopes of the mountains.

Rosie felt eager and aware, her senses stirred and stimulated by the man standing beside her as he surveyed this part of his realm.

Quietly she said, 'I know there's a lot more to Carathia than this valley, but it seems complete in itself.'

'One of my ancestors called it a fair land set above,' Gerd told her. 'And yes, Carathia's much bigger than the valley. The country wouldn't be nearly so prosperous without the coastal strip. It gives us easy access to the rest of the world, and makes us a very popular tourism destination. Then there are the agricultural lands further north, and the mines—all important.'

'But this is where the capital is, where the ruler lives; the heart of the country?'

'Its heart and its soul,' he said after a few moments. 'This is where those original Greek soldiers fought and settled and took wives, and it's always been the centre of power.'

'You're a real Carathian, aren't you?' she said quietly, wondering why this sudden realisation struck like a blow. 'Kelt might be a Duke here, but he's a Kiwi really—his heart belongs to New Zealand. You spent as much time in New Zealand as he did when you were younger, yet you're Carathian.'

'I knew from the time I was old enough to understand that this place was my destiny,' he pointed out. As though bored with the topic, he turned. 'Where would you like to sit? We can go inside, or they will set up a table for us out here.'

'Out here,' she said without hesitation. 'I want to enjoy every moment of this lovely place while I can. At home it's winter, and probably raining and a lot colder than this.'

'It rains here too,' he said, nodding to someone behind, 'quite often in summer. If you want a real summer you should go down to the coast. Or out to the islands. They're the true Mediterranean experience.'

Rosie said simply, 'I can't think of anything more lovely, or more Carathian, than this.'

She'd never see the fabled Adriatic coast of Carathia with its Greek and Roman ruins, the rows of vines across the white hills, the palms, the castles that defended each tiny sea-port, and the fishing boats with an eye painted on each bow for protection while they were out on the shimmering blue sea.

She'd never come back.

A waiter arrived bearing a silver tray and ice bucket; with ceremony he opened a bottle of champagne and poured out two glasses before presenting them.

Behind him Rosie could see people laying a table. It appeared she and Gerd were going to be the only people eating here. A swift frisson of excitement swept up through her and she had to resist the temptation to take a tiny, nervous sip of wine.

Gerd said, 'Are you cold? If you'd rather change your mind and eat inside we'll do that.'

'No, it's lovely here, perfect.' But just in case he got the wrong idea she said demurely, 'I've always wanted to dine in a mediaeval building with a handsome man and drink superb French champagne. It will be something to tell any grandchildren I might have. Will there be candles?'

His smile was narrow and sharp. 'Of course. Although it's a Renaissance building, to be accurate.' He held out his glass. 'Very well, then, a toast. We'll drink to your next visit here.'

Their glasses kissed, then separated. Rosie drank, trying to fully appreciate a wine that was clearly something special.

Common sense told her briskly that Gerd probably took French champagne as his due, and gave her the brash courage to say, 'I suppose Carathia's next big occasion will be the announcement of your engagement to Princess Serina.'

'You shouldn't believe everything you read in the media,' he said in a tone that told her she was trespassing.

Rosie's reckless heart contracted. For once unable to speak, she sent him a glance through her lashes.

Gerd's expression was unreadable, the handsome face aloof. 'She's only your age; far too young for me.'

The shameless flare of hope that had blazed fiercely for a few seconds died instantly. If the princess was too young for Gerd, so was she…

So much for her brave decision to stop yearning for him!

'Too young?' she demanded rashly. 'You're only twelve years older than I am. Does the princess think you're too old?'

His mouth thinned. 'We haven't discussed it.'

OK, stop right there! Although barely a muscle moved

in his handsome face, he couldn't have made it more plain that she'd overstepped the mark.

'So you don't think I'm too old for someone of your age?' Gerd asked, a steely note in his voice.

Embarrassed colour heated her skin. He couldn't know how painful this conversation was for her, and it was entirely her own fault.

Shrugging, she said, 'It depends entirely on the person, surely?'

'A very diplomatic answer,' he mocked. 'Restraint doesn't suit you.'

'I can be restrained when I want to,' she said loftily, only to flush at his mocking glance. Talk about a childish rejoinder!

'I'd noticed.' When she stared warily at him, he elaborated, 'Rosemary, you've always had beautiful manners and a kind heart. That's not the issue. Would you, for example, think twice about marrying a man twelve years older than you?'

'Not if I loved him.' He'd never know just how bitter the words were on her tongue. Desperate to change the subject, she said lamely, 'I'm sorry, I didn't intend to pry.' She paused, then admitted with a wry smile, 'Actually, of course I did. You and she have been photographed together a lot recently.'

'She and I know a lot of the same people. Gossip columnists are an over-excitable lot,' he said satirically. 'I'm surprised you read that rubbish. For your information, the family will be the first to know if and when I decide to announce my engagement.'

Clever Gerd. Although he hadn't confirmed any plans to marry, he hadn't denied them, either.

'Fair enough,' she said, pinning a smile to her lips. 'But you can't stop people from wondering. After all, you're probably the world's most eligible bachelor right now.'

'And the Press has to sell newspapers and magazines,' he said caustically, then carried the war into her territory. 'Kelt tells me that Aunt Eva is doing her best to marry you off.'

'Strangely enough when you consider the disaster her marriage was, that's exactly what she's up to, although it does seem her sole criterion for a good husband is the size of his bank balance.' She gave him a cool glance. 'So far I haven't been tempted by the men she's introduced to me.'

Gerd looked down at her. The fading sun set shimmering little fires in her hair and sprinkled her perfect skin with gold dust. There had been no cynicism in her tone, merely rueful resignation.

'So who is the current lover?' he probed.

As a child her face had been mobile, every emotion displayed for the world to read. Since then she'd learned control; the Rosemary he'd known, the girl he'd kissed, had been banished, her place taken by this glossy, self-assured woman.

Her brows rose. 'Mother's?'

'Yours. Anyone I know?'

'Nobody at the moment,' she said lightly, her expression giving nothing away.

Frustration tightened Gerd's lips. She was so young—far too young to be making any lifetime promises—but her soft, sensuously curved lips, the conscious awareness in her eyes, her sophistication, meant she was no stranger to passion.

So? He'd known that ever since he'd kissed her. And if her ardent response hadn't convinced him of it, seeing her in Kelt's arms the next morning would have. The memory of those kisses he'd witnessed still burned like acid. Growing up in the care of a woman whose chaotic search for love had invariably ended in disillusion must have given Rosemary a distorted view of what a relationship could be between a man and a woman.

Reining in a cold, baseless anger, Gerd wondered for possibly the thousandth time if it had been Kelt who'd taught her the full depths of her passion.

He'd never mentioned them to his brother, not even a few hours after their kiss, when Kelt had issued a veiled warning cloaked in friendly banter but making sure Gerd understood that he was watching out for Rosemary. Ashamed of the loss of control that had prompted his desire the previous night, Gerd had responded with an icy aloofness that had convinced Kelt he had no intention of breaking the girl's heart.

He'd seen very little of his brother since then. Partly, he admitted, because he hated the thought of Kelt being Rosemary's first lover.

If he had been, it hadn't lasted long. Shortly after Gerd had returned to Carathia Hani had appeared, and Kelt had gone under like a drowning man.

It would be bitterly ironic if he'd broken Rosemary's heart, setting her on her mother's path of short, futile relationships that had no chance of surviving.

Was she still longing for Kelt? There had definitely

been something in her eyes, in her voice, when she'd watched Kelt dance with Hani.

His instinctive distaste was backed by another, much less civilised emotion. Jealousy...

Gerd looked over her head. 'The table's ready for us,' he said brusquely. 'Come and sit down.'

She gave him a curious glance, but responded with cool friendliness, just as she had all week, treating him like a much older brother. To his intense irritation she kept it up while they ordered and settled into a discussion about the parlous state of the planet. He admired her quick intelligence, but he missed the sparkling challenge he'd only glimpsed since she'd arrived in Carathia.

Gerd despised himself for being both intrigued and disturbed. Over the past few days he hadn't been able to stop himself noting the way other men had looked at her, responding to her subtle, understated sensuousness.

His sharp, involuntary reaction to those speculative glances had angered him. He'd had to stop himself from moving in to—to what?

Establish some sort of claim?

Reluctantly he admitted it. Of course his intervention hadn't been necessary; her experience showed in the way she'd skilfully parried any advances.

He'd wanted her at eighteen, but it was impossible. He was no debaucher of innocent girls.

But now...now she was no longer innocent.

While they'd been talking darkness had fallen—thick, all-encompassing, enclosing them in an intimate circle of candlelight, yet Rosie sensed a distance in him, an aloofness that chilled her. An upward glance revealed that he was looking at her, his eyes remote behind the thick screen of his lashes.

He was watching her mouth.

Tension shafted through her, bringing with it a fierce delight. She'd seen desire often enough to recognise it. In spite of his formidable restraint, Gerd was attracted to her.

Rosie's heart clamped in her breast.

So? she thought, trying to tamp down the unwanted tumult of excitement. Desire was common coin; it meant nothing beyond the swift heat of passion. She'd always been repulsed by men whose only interest in her was physical.

But this was different; this was Gerd...

Don't go there! Doing her best to be sophisticated, she warned herself that Gerd was very much a man, and so just as capable of feeling meaningless passion as her rejected would-be lovers.

That hateful thought prompted her to remark tartly, 'Pondering matters of state, Gerd? Or should I call you Your Royal Highness now?'

Their eyes clashed, his hard and more than a little intimidating. 'Only if you say it in Carathian. And even then, only if you're a Carathian citizen.'

'So what do people who are neither call you?'

'My family and friends call me Gerd.'

'Then I'll stick to that,' she said jauntily, adding with a wry smile, 'even though I'm neither family nor friend.'

She didn't know what she expected from him after that—a smoothly bland statement that she was both, perhaps. But he leaned back in his chair and regarded her steadily, his handsome face sardonic.

For some reason an erratic pulse beat high in Rosie's throat; she had to clasp one hand around the stem of the champagne glass to stop herself from covering that betraying little hollow, but she could do nothing about the exhilarating rush of adrenalin that charged through her.

Lazily he said, 'We've had this conversation before. Since you're Alex's half-sister, I consider you to be very much part of the family even though there is no blood connection. As for being friends, do you think a man and a woman can be nothing more than friends?'

'Some men, some women,' she returned. 'It's not impossible.'

His brows lifted. 'Let's be specific, then. Do you think you and I could be friends?'

Was he flirting with her? Tantalised by the thought, Rosie struggled to achieve the right throwaway tone. 'It doesn't seem likely. Friendships need to be worked at, and how often we seen each other in the past three years? I don't think we can call ourselves friends. Friendly acquaintances, possibly.'

There, that should show him she didn't want any sort of *flirtatious* relationship with him. Darn it, she was trying to get him out of her system! Encouraging this sort of half-bantering innuendo was not the way to do that.

'An innocuous description.' But a raw edge in his voice sent surreptitious little shivers the length of her spine, warned her it might not be wise to take his words at face value.

A waiter arrived with the first course, a cold soup, and while they drank it Gerd steered the conversation into much safer channels.

Relieved, Rosie followed his lead, keeping her gaze away from those darkly golden eyes, that fascinating mouth. Only to discover she couldn't stop looking at his hands—lean, long-fingered and smoothly assured.

Little quivers tightened inside her as she found herself wondering what they'd feel like on her skin. She swallowed hastily and told herself to be sensible. She knew exactly what they felt like; when he'd kissed her he'd slid his hands across her back, causing a shuddery delight to riot through her.

Stop thinking about it! She forced herself to be bright, to wait a second before she spoke, and to restrict herself to impersonal glances and manufactured smiles.

By the time dinner ended she was as taut and tightly coiled as an over-wound spring. There wasn't the usual business with credit cards, and she bit her lip to stop asking how such payments were managed. Did the restaurant send a bill to the palace?

The same car met them again, with the same anonymous security man beside the chauffeur. Rosie sank back into the seat, clipping her seat belt across to form a fragile barrier between her and Gerd.

Stupid, because of course he wouldn't pounce!

Gazing out of the window, she said the first thing that came into her head. 'I like modern buildings, but I have to admit these old houses with their carvings and oriel windows and studded doors have something that makes me wish New Zealand had a longer history.'

'The novelty, probably.' He sounded distant, glad that

the evening had finished. 'You're used to houses built of timber. The fact that in Carathia stone has always been the cheapest and most common material might make the buildings here more romantic.'

Rosie ignored a little jab of pain. 'Could be,' she agreed, and lapsed into silence as they drove through the still-busy streets and up the hill to the palace, huge and dramatically lit on the hill.

'It's so big,' she ventured, gazing at the classical splendour of it. 'Did the ancestor who built this have a particularly large family?'

'A particularly large sense of his own importance,' Gerd told her astringently. 'One of his barons married a woman from southern Italy who found the family's ancient castle intolerably cold. She must have been very beautiful and he must have been besotted, because he razed it and used the stone to build a mansion. Not to be outdone, the then Grand Duke had the original castle here demolished so he could build a much bigger, more grand palace than his vassal.'

'To the great relief of everyone who followed him onto the throne, I'm sure,' she returned cheerfully. 'I love castles—they're grim and powerful and evocative of history and passion and treachery and chivalry, but I'll bet the reason they're mostly in ruins now is because they were so uncomfortable.'

The car drew up inside the palace courtyard. 'Comfort over romance, Rosemary?'

Uneasily aware of his brief smile as he spoke, she said, 'Absolutely.' And it wasn't entirely a lie.

As they walked towards the door Gerd said, 'A nightcap?'

CHAPTER FOUR

COMMON sense told Rosie to make her excuses and her escape as quickly as she could with dignity.

But if she'd listened to common sense when Gerd asked her to dinner she'd have missed out on the bittersweetness of the evening. From now on she'd only see Gerd in photographs. The knowledge ached through her, summoning a kind of desperation, a need to hug each precious moment to her breast.

Think of it as a final goodbye, she told herself with bleak realism. Without a tremor she said, 'Thank you, I'd enjoy that.'

In his private sitting room he poured drinks while she examined the room. This was not the bigger one where he'd entertained the family, but a smaller, more intimate affair, furnished quite casually. Her gaze ranged from the huge sofas that befitted a man of his height to some exquisite glassware in a cabinet, and she made a soft sound of pleasure.

'From Venice,' he said, following the direction of her gaze as he handed her the drink. 'The Venetians ruled most of this coast at one time.'

'Did they conquer Carathia?'

'No, but they demanded a yearly tribute—wine and silver from the mines.'

'The glass is beautiful, such glorious colours. I didn't know there were silver mines here.'

'They've been worked out for a couple of centuries, but they were what made Carathia prosperous in the Middle Ages.'

Rosie sipped the white wine he'd given her. A silky, subtly sweet liquor, it breathed the scent of flowers. 'This smells like spring. And tastes like it too. Is it from here?'

'Yes.' Grim-faced, he looked down at her, and in a voice she'd never heard before said, 'I chose it because you always remind me of spring.'

Rosie froze, silenced by a fierce rush of adrenalin. She looked up into glittering golden eyes as a heady recklessness clamoured through her, a torrent both languorous and without mercy, sweet as honey and dangerous. Through the drumbeat of her pulse she tightened her shaking fingers around the glass. The voluptuous appetite Gerd roused with his kisses all those years ago blazed into open need.

She began to tremble.

Narrowed eyes gleaming, he took the almost untouched wine from her and set the glass on a table. Rosie's heart gave a great leap and the breath stopped in her throat. Heat pounded through her, softening her bones, banishing any coherent thoughts in a widening surge of hunger.

Yet as Gerd lifted her hands to his lips, she managed to croak, 'This is not a good idea, Gerd.'

'Have you a better one?' he asked deeply.

Shivers chased themselves over her skin, through every wakening cell in her body. 'I don't know—I just don't really think...' she said in confusion, the words slurring when he kissed the jumping pulse in one wrist.

His mouth was hot and demanding, lingering over the fine skin. Rosie swallowed to ease her dry throat. There was something she had to say, but she couldn't remember what.

Still holding her gaze, he held her hands to his chest so that the open palms rested above his heart. Its rapid beat echoed her own turbulent pulse, thundering a primitive call.

Rosie closed her eyes, but that made things worse; without sight every other sense was sharpened. She could hear his breath, hard and fast as though he'd been running, and his faint, masculine scent teased her nostrils— evocative, compelling.

Desperate, she forced up her lashes and held his gaze, wincing at the arrogant jut of his jaw and the golden glints in his eyes, the eyes of a predator.

She should be terrified.

She wasn't.

But something had to be said.

'Princess Serina?' she muttered almost pleadingly.

He told her harshly, 'I've made no commitment to her or to any other woman. She is not expecting a proposal from me.'

Rosie struggled to articulate a further question, but he kissed the unformed words from her lips, and she surrendered to desire so intense her knees buckled. Gerd's arms tightened around her. She gasped when he picked her up and carried her, mouth on mouth, across the room, sinking onto one of the big sofas without releasing her.

The kisses turned shockingly erotic when he bent her head back across his shoulder and explored her sweet depths with a torrid passion. Dimly, vaguely, Rosie wondered if she should have run while she had the chance.

Too late now. His slow, drugging kisses summoned a wildly incandescent response from every cell in her body and she had never felt so safe.

Yet never been in such danger...

Gerd lifted his head and scrutinised her face, penetrating eyes gleaming between dark lashes, the angular framework of his handsome face suddenly far more prominent. 'If you don't want this tell me right now, before it's too late.'

Rosie dragged breath into her famished lungs. Disconnected thoughts tumbled in freefall around her brain, fleeting scraps so coloured by emotion she couldn't assemble them into any coherent order.

Finally she managed, 'Why?'

Closing his eyes, he said in a rough voice, 'Rosemary, I've wanted you since I first kissed you, but you were far too young.' Catching her unawares, he opened his eyes again, fixing her with a fierce, unguarded gaze that set more nerves jangling. 'And now you're grown-up, but it has to be what you want too.'

His words jerked Rosie upwards. Mouth tight, eyes blazing, she surveyed his ruthless face.

It was too cruel of him to kiss her like that, as though she was the most important thing in his life, as though he'd longed for her just as fiercely as she'd craved him, and then let his damned principles get in the way.

Furious, she exploded, 'Of *course* I want you—I've wanted you since I understood what wanting is.'

He said harshly, 'You deserve more than a one-night stand.'

For some strange reason his words strengthened her resolution. She met his gaze with boldness. 'So do you.'

His chest lifted and she saw wry laughter gleam in the golden eyes.

And something else, she realised, her heart picking up speed once more. Determination, as though he'd come to some turning point and now saw the way ahead.

'So perhaps we will forget about it being just one night,' he said. In a voice without any inflection he asked, 'What is your decision?'

'Why do *I* have to decide?' she demanded.

He gave her a taut, narrow smile. 'You know why.' He held out his hand. Slowly she put her hand into his keeping. Against the tanned strength of his, hers looked fragile, almost lost.

He wrapped his fingers around hers and said, 'Pull.'

'I don't have to.' Her stupid hand was shaking, and she fought back an unregenerate sizzle of excitement. 'I know you're stronger than I am.'

'That's why *you* decide,' he told her inflexibly.

Clearly, he wasn't going to change his mind. Without thinking she hauled back. Instantly his fingers closed around hers, holding them in a firm grip that didn't hurt.

And then he let her go. In a voice as uncompromising as that grip had been, he said, 'Make up your mind, Rosemary.'

Awash with a hunger that screamed for satisfaction, Rosie forced herself to think. Part of the hold he had on her had to be simple frustration because she'd never made love. In her dreams it was wonderful, transcendental, but she'd listened to enough friends to understand it needn't necessarily be like that.

So if she experienced sex with Gerd chances were she could rid herself of this fruitless desire.

Or it might make things worse—give life to a craving she couldn't control.

But that had already happened. Hell, because of this man she was still a virgin!

Be logical, she told herself almost beseechingly. A long-distance friendship was difficult enough to sustain; a long-distance love affair—one based only on sex— would be even more difficult.

Eventually it must burn out, and when it did she'd be free of the lingering hangover of her adolescent passion for him.

She said, 'I—all right, now that we know that this… this *need* is mutual, why not just follow it and see what happens?'

His mouth tightened. 'Be sophisticated and adult about it?'

'Is there anything wrong with that?' she demanded, challenging him directly. 'It's better than being foolish and juvenile, surely? We're both adults. We both know this can't go anywhere, so why not take what we can from it and enjoy it and when it dies remember it without regret?'

Gerd smiled, but his eyes were coolly watchful, and

she had no idea what he felt when he said, 'If that's what you want, then that is the way it will happen.'

But he made no movement to kiss her again, and an icy chill of panic gripped her. Had she repelled him, even disgusted him?

And then he smiled and said softly, 'I suspect you're every man's dream mistress, Rosemary—no strings, no commitment, no future planned. Just the promise of sex whenever we want it, wherever we want it.' His voice deepened. 'However we want it.'

'Oh, there's going to be some sort of commitment,' she told him, hoping she sounded as confident as her words. But she needed to get something straight, although her heart constricted when she said, 'Until we call a halt I'll be faithful to you, and I'll expect the same from you.'

The dark head bent in an autocratic nod. 'Very well, then, it's a deal.'

The words were blunt, as blunt as hers had been, she reminded herself.

'It's a deal,' she whispered, and held out her hand.

His mouth was a thin line, strangely ruthless, as they shook hands. But it gentled when he lifted her hand to his mouth and kissed her fingertips.

The sensuous caress sent more wanton excitement tingling through Rosie. And then he bent his head and kissed her again, and his mouth took her into that realm where thought and logic no longer mattered, where the only reality was Gerd's passion and her abandoned response.

But even as she yielded she wondered how he might react if he realised she'd never done this before.

It didn't matter. His kisses stoked the fires that had

been smouldering so long; for the second time in her life real desire slammed through her, a relentless, consuming source of pleasure and anticipation that banished any apprehension.

When Gerd found the hollow at the base of her throat and kissed the feverish pulse there, she stiffened and gave a soft, involuntary groan.

'You even smell of spring,' he said, his voice low and impeded. 'All flowers and sweetness and energy...'

Rosie pushed his shirt back and kissed his shoulder, her mouth open and seeking. He tasted like every dream she'd ever had—a sexy mix of challenge and charisma and power, an earthy flavour that was Gerd alone, made from his body, the true essence of the man.

To her astonished delight, she felt him tense, and then his mouth moved to the curve of her breast.

Breath locking in her throat, she waited for the revulsion she usually felt, the sense of being invaded that always before had had her calling an abrupt halt.

It didn't come. When he kissed her she understood the true meaning of longing; tautly expectant, her breasts ached with voluptuous hunger that only he could ease.

But he lifted his head. She had only a moment to endure the cold chill of rejection before he began to push aside the ties that held up her dress.

'Am I likely to wreck this pretty thing by doing this?'

Gerd's raw voice only added to the reckless clamour in her blood. 'No.'

She wondered at her voice, husky and slow, so that the syllable flowed into the silence in the room like liquid honey.

'Hold up your arms.'

Silently, eyes enormous and smoky in her face, she obeyed, and he eased the material over her head, dropping it over the arm of the sofa.

The dress had a built-in bra and slip, so beneath it she wore nothing but narrow briefs. To her horror Rosie realised she was blushing, the colour burning up from her bared breasts.

Too shy to look at him, she averted her face, freezing when he curved his hand around her jaw. Her lashes drooped; fascinated, shocked, she hardly breathed while he surveyed what he'd uncovered. His expression didn't change, but she felt a subtle alteration in him, a kind of charged awareness that ratcheted up her tension so that hunger exploded like a pain inside her, demanding and elemental, a force that consumed her entirely.

'Your skin is like silk,' he said.

The words sounded rough, yet she didn't make the mistake of thinking he was angry. She'd never imagined that Gerd could look at her with such…such intensity, as though she was something infinitely rare and precious, something he didn't dare touch.

A reckless shiver shook her. And she'd never felt so exposed, lying almost naked across his lap while he was still fully clothed.

Now what? For a horrified moment she thought she'd actually said the words.

'I have to get undressed too.' He spoke with harsh precision, as though he'd had to concentrate on what he was saying, and began to undo his shirt.

Rosie stayed still, her eyes on the dark, long fingers against the white material. She forced herself to take a breath, listening as it came through her lips, hearing the beating of her heart heavy and fast in her ears, the taste of Gerd in her mouth.

Should she tell him this was all new to her?

No.

It didn't mean anything, or perhaps it meant too much. She didn't want to load him with the burden of her virginity. Blurting it out would somehow make the fact that she was untouched more important than this languid, golden tide of passion, so intense it closed her throat.

Mutely, her heart hammering in her breast, she watched as Gerd shrugged free of the shirt and tossed it over her dress.

Rosie hesitated, but desire persuaded her to stretch out a tentative hand and trace with splayed fingers the path of the scroll of hair across his powerful chest. Startled, she registered the tension of muscles beneath that lightest of exploratory touches, and for the first time a tinge of apprehension shadowed her headstrong physical longing.

Perhaps he sensed her involuntary fear. His kiss was tender and gentle, only deepening when he felt the wildfire response she could no longer control.

And by the time his mouth found the pleading tip of her breast she was again on fire for him, writhing restlessly as he showed her just how responsive her breasts were to his caress.

When eventually he said in a thickened, harsh voice, 'Not here, I think,' she stared at him in bewilderment, her eyes huge and dark in her face.

His smile hard and savage, an elemental claim of possession, he eased her off him before getting to his feet and picking her up.

'You're just the right size for this,' he said, and snatched another kiss before striding across the room.

Dazedly Rosie registered that the room he took her to was his bedroom. Eyes fixed on Gerd's hard-hewn face, she felt the cool kiss of sheets on her bare back.

He bent to remove her sandals, his fingers stroking up her leg. Rosie's breath locked in her throat.

But he straightened, and efficiently stripped off the rest of his clothes. Instinctively Rosie's lashes fluttered down. It took all of her willpower to force them up again; this might be the only time she had with him, and she wanted to see, wanted to know...

Storing up memories is dangerous, the last sensible part of her brain told her. Resolutely, she dismissed the bleak prophecy, allowing her gaze to linger.

Because Gerd was magnificently male, enough to dazzle any woman, tall and powerfully muscled, the dim light from the other room glossing his bronze skin to reveal more than the darkness hid. Without volition she held out her hand.

He took it, but didn't obey her silent plea. Instead, he said, 'Who am I?'

A frown pleated her brows. 'You know who you are,' she said uncertainly.

'Then call me by my name.'

'Gerd,' she said unevenly.

'Is that all?'

She didn't know what he wanted from her, but she said huskily, 'Gerd is all that interests me. Your surname comes from the past; Gerd is now.'

He raised her hand to his mouth and kissed the palm, then let his teeth graze the mount of Venus beneath her thumb. 'Rosemary,' he said, making her name an act of possession.

The tiny caress was more erotic than any previous kiss; her lithe body twisted of its own accord and on a low, dark laugh he came down beside her and gathered her into his arms and pinned her against his lean, powerful body and kissed her breath—and every thought—out of existence.

But even then he let her go and turned away. 'Just a moment,' he said quietly.

Hot-cheeked, she realised what he was doing. It was a measure of the enchantment he'd cast over her that she'd forgotten completely about the possibility of pregnancy!

And when he turned back everything was all right again, because this was Gerd, and she wanted him beyond—oh, beyond hope, beyond fear, almost beyond desire.

He wooed her with kisses and caresses, and a knowledge that could only be the result, she'd realise later, of vast experience. So lost in her wild response that she didn't care, Rosie forgot her total lack of experience and followed his lead, caressing him as he did her, until finally her body twisted against him, hips thrusting as she sought something else—something more than this exquisite, desperate pleasure.

Voice gravelly and raw, he said, 'Time?'

'Yes,' she whispered, 'oh, yes, please…'

But he didn't immediately move over her; instead he stroked her skin from her throat to the juncture of her legs, his skilled, questing fingers firing her anticipation into a fever.

Only then did he take her, thrusting past the fragile barrier and claiming her in that most primal of all embraces.

Gasping with the shock, Rosie clamped muscles she hadn't known she possessed.

Gerd froze, his eyes glittering, his chest lifting while he fought for air. 'What the *hell*?'

Her hips jerked upwards. It was so near, so close—yet not close enough. She slid importunate hands across his sleek back, pulling him down so that she could move frantically against him.

Although she could feel his resistance it didn't last; almost immediately he responded, his big body fiercely attuned to hers as he sent her further and further along the path towards an elusive goal that retreated and advanced in slow, erotic waves.

A delirious yearning gripped her with silken talons, until at last the sensation became so intense she gave a gasping sob as it overwhelmed her, hurtling her beyond some invisible border into another dimension where all that counted was the perfect ecstasy that surged through her.

Almost immediately Gerd too found that place and yielded to its untamed rapture, head flung back, body taut with barely controlled energy until repletion overtook him.

Dazed by exhausted pleasure, Rosie looped her arms around him, pretending, oh, pretending such *foolish* things as their breaths harmonised and slowly, slowly they coasted down that long slope to reality.

Gerd turned on his side and hooked his finger under

her chin, tilting her face so that he could scan it, raptor's eyes metallic, like frozen fire.

He said something—from its tone, an oath—in Carathian, and as her eyes widened rasped in English, 'Damn it, why didn't you tell me?'

Rosie couldn't think of anything sensible to say. How could she have been so, so *abandoned*, so lost in his arms she'd neglected the one thing her mother had impressed on her—to make sure there would be no possibility of a child?

After several moments of taut silence he asked coldly, 'Are you using any sort of protection at all?'

She refused to lie. 'No, and I didn't need to, did I? You did.'

'I might not have,' he ground out. 'What would you have done, then?'

'OK, so I behaved like an idiot,' she said, her lovely glow dissipating into desolation under the icy onslaught of his anger. 'Probably because I was certain you'd be more careful.'

He swore again and let her go as though she disgusted him. 'And why didn't you tell me you were a virgin?'

Sick at heart, Rosie angled her chin away from him. It took every ounce of courage she possessed to say in a steady voice, 'It wasn't important.'

For some reason that made him even more angry. 'Not *important*?' he snarled. 'Of course it was important; if you didn't think so you'd have leapt into bed with any one of the men you've been connected to.'

Again there didn't seem to be an answer. To tell him the truth—that if she couldn't have him she wanted nobody—was out of the question, so she shrugged. 'For heaven's sake, it's not an issue. I've always done what I thought was right for me.'

He leaned back against the pillows. Rosie glanced sideways, saw his arrogant profile silhouetted against the light from the open door, and in spite of everything her pulse started to quicken again; he looked magnificent, big and handsome and furious.

Hastily she turned her face away again.

He enquired icily, 'How could making love with me be right for you?'

'I don't know,' she said without thinking, and because that made her seem a complete fool she went on quickly, 'Oh, stop being so—so *macho* about this. I just didn't think it was necessary to tell you.' Colour heated her skin and she finished in a smoky voice, 'Besides, I wasn't thinking clearly at all—not after that first kiss, anyway.'

His eyes narrowed. 'I'm delighted to hear that,' he said with chilling courtesy. 'But condoms are not fool-proof.'

Well, of course that was what he was worried about. What else?

A sense of self-preservation forced her to hide her bleakness with an airy tone. 'I can easily see a doctor and get protection. But if you want to call things off, I'll understand.'

After all, he'd thought he'd be embarking on an affair with a woman of experience. Possibly he found her caresses incredibly gauche and dull.

Her words were followed by an edged silence before he turned his head and surveyed the length of her body. Rosie's skin prickled at that slow, almost insulting scrutiny, but deep inside her a humiliating heat began to smoulder into life.

'No,' he said silkily. 'We made a deal, remember? That we'd see where this goes.'

'I—yes, but you thought you were dealing with someone who knew what she was doing. Your reaction tells me you're not happy—'

'Only because you didn't tell me,' he interrupted, running a deliberate finger around the ivory curve of one breast, the light, tantalising caress tightening her skin and stirring a swift, heated response. 'If you had I'd have been more gentle.'

On a swift indrawn breath she whispered, 'I didn't need gentle. Are you sure you don't mind?'

'Mind?' he said deeply. 'I was just startled. And delighted. Why should I complain about your charming lack of experience? As I said before, you're every man's dream. No responsibility, and the pleasure of transforming that sensuous innocence of yours into knowledge. I'm holding you to our deal.'

Something about him made her move uneasily even as her heartbeat began to race. On an indrawn breath, she muttered, 'Only if you're sure?'

The words strangled in her throat when he bent his black head to trace with his mouth the path his finger had taken.

Against her skin he said, 'I'm very sure. It will be my pleasure to teach you.'

That uneasy feeling deepened until he lifted his head and said blandly, 'But not tonight. You'll probably be too tender.'

Rosie opened her mouth to protest, only to be surprised by a yawn.

With an ironic smile Gerd got up and gently pulled her to her feet. 'Besides,' he said, 'there are things to be discussed, and tonight is obviously not the time to do that. When you're dressed I'll take you to your room.'

Scrambling into her clothes, Rosie tried very hard to emulate his casual acceptance of the situation. But when he left her at her door, his kiss started off chastely, only to transform within seconds into something much more potent.

However, he lifted his head and stepped back, his expression giving nothing away. Rosie looked mutely at him, so awash with longing she couldn't summon any words.

'Goodnight,' he said evenly, and left her.

Half an hour later, her evening regime completed, Rosie lay in the big bed and tried to make sense of what had happened. He'd probably thought she'd slept with dozens of men, she thought acidly, before a second, more bewildering thought occurred to her.

Uneasily she turned and punched the pillow. Things— her life—had changed so fundamentally she didn't know how to cope.

It felt as though a balance had shifted, and their love-making had somehow given Gerd a power over her he hadn't possessed before.

No, that was foolish. She was the same person; well, almost the same, apart from knowing a lot more about sex than she had only a few hours ago.

And it had been wonderful, she thought dreamily; no matter what happened, she'd always have that.

He'd been masterful and skilled, passionate and fiercely tender, and she'd thrilled to every minute of it...

Smiling, she drifted off to sleep.

And woke the next morning to a slightly achy body and a much more practical frame of mind, half-bewildered yet still excited by what had happened the night before.

She glanced at her watch and gave a muffled yelp. 'Packing,' she muttered, leaping out of bed.

Most of the morning had disappeared, leaving her with practically no time to pack. She hadn't even thought of it last night, but Gerd hadn't said anything about her staying, so presumably he expected her to leave as planned.

When she'd arrived her luggage had been unpacked by a maid, and she'd been told to ring if she needed anything. She hadn't, and she didn't know whether she should leave a tip, or how such things were organised in the palace.

She should have asked Hani.

It was less stressful to worry about that than face the fact that she had no idea what was going to happen with Gerd. Did he want her to stay? Would he suggest a date for their next meeting?

The past week had shown her that his life was organised well ahead. He hadn't suggested she stay in Carathia, but he'd talked about contraception—surely that meant he intended some sort of ongoing relationship?

A knock on her door whirled her about; she hesitated, then called out, 'Come in.'

It was Gerd, tall and stern and aloof. 'Come with me.'

Chilled, she accompanied him into the room she'd been in the previous night. A glance at the big sofa brought a swift bloom of heat to her skin, but that soon vanished when he spoke.

'I've cancelled your flight home.'

CHAPTER FIVE

SHEER astonishment silenced Rosie—but only for a second. 'You had no right,' she flashed.

Face impassive, Gerd shrugged. 'Did you want to go back to New Zealand?'

The one question she didn't want to answer. After a deep breath she stated emphatically, 'That was my decision to make, not yours. I'm not one of your subjects, to be told what to do.'

He shrugged as though her protest meant nothing. 'It's done now. Last night you spoke of seeing a doctor about contraception. She'll be here in half an hour.' He paused, then said, 'But if you want to return to New Zealand I'll organise a flight for you—a much more comfortable one than riding cattle class in a jumbo jet.'

He smiled, and her heart twisted, anger draining away under the sensuous impact. Defying its effect, she repeated, 'But the decision was mine to make, not yours.'

'Was it the wrong decision?'

'I…' She took a deep breath and admitted, 'No.'

His brows shot up, then his expression relaxed. 'Kelt has called me an arrogant bastard fairly frequently—perhaps he's right. What do *you* want to do?'

Uncertainly she said, 'I don't know.' Her lips trembled;

startled, she blinked at the hot sting of tears and swallowed hard. 'Oh, damn!'

She stiffened when Gerd covered the two paces between them, but when he took her in his arms she melted, resting her forehead against his disarmingly broad shoulder.

'I'm not used to anything like this,' she admitted into his shirt. 'And you are.'

'I've told you before, don't believe the gossip columnists,' he said crisply.

'Even if only half of what's been written is true it means you're a whole lot more experienced than I am,' she pointed out miserably.

He held her away from him, his face closed against her. 'I have had lovers, yes. Not very many, and none of them have been casual.'

That hurt too; she didn't dare let him see how much. 'Go on.'

'I shall not tell you about them—it would be a betrayal of trust. Last night you laid down conditions—conditions I accepted. As long as we are together you do not need to worry about any other women.'

When she said nothing he held her a little further away and scanned her face with astute, penetrating eyes. 'Do you believe me?'

'I—yes.' She hesitated, then went on, 'Yes, of course I believe you. It's just that I don't know anything about *being together*.'

He smiled, and drew her against him again, holding her with wonderful gentleness. 'Perhaps I should have expected some uncertainty, but it surprises me that the Rosemary who has always been so outspoken and confident should show such wariness. So, am I forgiven for assuming that you would prefer to stay here than fly to New Zealand?'

Rosemary suspected that she'd forgive him anything. The thought shocked her; she had a feeling he might ride roughshod over her if she didn't lay down boundaries.

What really alarmed her was that she didn't want to.

'Rosemary?'

She admitted, 'Yes, provided it doesn't happen again. And I promise that you won't have to worry about any other men, either.'

His face hardened. 'So, we understand each other.'

And he kissed her, a fleeting kiss on her forehead that somehow appeased her more than a passionate one would have, and drew her arm through his as he walked her towards the door.

He said, 'I have several more days of official and ceremonial engagements, but after that I'm taking a month's holiday at a villa I own on an island off the coast. If you don't mind being by yourself for four days it would be best if you went ahead to the villa.'

Rosie's heart chilled. 'Why?'

His face was unreadable. 'If you appear in the media as my latest mistress the paparazzi will be around you like flies.'

Wincing at being so casually described—and at the thought of the media scrummage that might ensue—she said, 'I see.'

Gerd said, 'I remember how you loved staying at the bach at Kiwinui, so you should enjoy the villa.' He smiled and dropped a swift kiss on her mouth, straightening far too soon. 'And four days is not very long.'

But they were the longest days in Rosie's life. Oh, the island was a dream—the fabled coast she'd been so sure she'd never see. White houses cupped a small harbour where gaily painted fishing boats puttered in and out. Olives shimmered silver-green on the hillsides, and vines braided the slopes. The salt of the sea mingled with the perfumes of flowers blooming in the gardens.

And the villa—surely a misnomer for such a big house—dreamed away the summer days beneath a sky as blue and potent as the sea that mimicked it.

But Rosie was lonely, racked by an aching emptiness that frightened her. Always before she'd enjoyed her own company; now she spent the days waiting, longing for the call Gerd made every day on the secure telephone.

Not that he murmured love words to her; a smile quirked her lips as she sprayed herself with more sunscreen. She just couldn't imagine Gerd mouthing sweet nothings.

And there was no *love* in their relationship. Reduced to the shameful truth, it was just a mutual itch that had irritated them for years. Now was their chance to sate it.

Once that was done they'd go their separate ways.

Even as an adolescent she'd known that there could never be a future for them. Gerd's life had been mapped out for him from birth; eventually he'd marry a princess of the right age and temperament, and they'd have children to carry on the succession.

He'd made it obvious she was the wrong age, and she'd always known she had the wrong temperament—a conviction strengthened by watching Hani, with her gracious charm, and Princess Serina, who'd seemed to know everyone and find just the right word for them.

On the third day Rosie leaned back in the hammock and frowned up through the branches of the big tree that shaded it. Tomorrow evening Gerd would come.

'So you'd better face the facts,' she said aloud. However distasteful they were, she needed to have them clear in her mind before he arrived and scrambled it with his smile, his touch...

They'd have their month and then she'd go back to New Zealand and find herself a job, save like crazy and one day—with any luck in the not-too-distant future— she'd buy her florist's shop.

A faint buzzing lifted her head. Frowning, she scanned the sky, blinking into the sun. A helicopter—coming this way and descending.

Gerd? Today?

Wild excitement pulsed through her, and an overwhelming shyness. She almost fell out of the hammock and stood tensely waiting as the chopper dropped down onto the helipad behind the villa.

It seemed an age before he came striding out of the house, tall and dark and dominating. Her heart drummed feverishly, and she thought, *Oh, you idiot! This is not lust. There's nothing casual about this at all—you're in love with him. Real, now-and-forever love!*

How had it happened? Three lonely days shouldn't have altered everything.

Of course it hadn't. She'd been in love with him all along, at least ever since he'd kissed her those long, empty years ago. Even though she hadn't recognised it, no other man had been able to break through the shield that was her love for Gerd.

The balance of power had shifted even further in his favour. If he ever found out, what would he do?

'Rosemary.'

Just the one word, but her world brightened into a brilliance she'd never known as he came up to her and bent over her, enclosing her in a hard, almost painful hug.

He didn't kiss her. For long seconds he simply held her against his powerful body, embracing her as though this fierce closeness was something he'd been craving since he last saw her.

'Miss me?' His voice was rough, almost harsh.

'Like crazy.' Was that her, that breathless, hopeful tone? Hopeless! Infusing her voice with lazy laughter, she asked, 'How about you?'

'Every minute, every second, all day, every night.' It sounded like a vow. 'Which is why I'm here before time.'

He found her mouth in a kiss so hot and urgent her knees buckled. His arms tightened even further, and he lifted her and sank into the hammock, pulling her on top so that she felt the intimate hardness of him beneath her.

Sensation roared through her, a rich, unfulfilled flood. When they broke the kiss she explored his face with her lips until he groaned and muttered, 'Stop this right now before I unman myself. Maria is expecting us for lunch in five minutes.'

Rosie laughed and cuddled against him. 'You said it would be four days before you could get here.'

He shrugged. 'As I said, I got away earlier.'

Something in his voice alerted Rosie—a reserve that sent an uneasy quiver along her sensitised nerves. She asked quietly, 'Is everything OK?'

Stretched along his lean body, she felt an infinitesimal tightening. Concerned, she raised her head so she could look into his eyes.

But they were shuttered against her, although he said smoothly, 'Everything's fine—and much better now I'm here.'

'Good,' she said, and scrambled off him, wary once more.

He let her go and got out in a lithe movement, then held the side of the hammock steady as she wriggled free and stood up.

Although the realisation might be newborn, she realised now she'd loved Gerd as long as she could remember—an unrecognised, unwanted love, always there like a steady fire, as much a part of her as her eyes and her voice and her heart.

Gerd didn't love her. OK, so he hadn't actually come out and said so, but he'd been quite straightforward about the situation, and she—fool that she'd been, unable to recognise her true feelings—had accepted his terms.

She'd even been confident she could deal with the inevitably bitter ending. Dear heaven, she must have been crazy...

She should have taken the coward's way out and run all the way back to New Zealand, but it was too late now.

Hard on that thought came another. He must never know.

It would be dishonourable to do anything else, because he couldn't give her the love she longed for.

She could cope with anything rather than pity.

So she had to make sure he never glimpsed her love; she'd have to monitor every word, every action, to keep him from guessing her secret.

He reached out a lazy hand for her, then let it drop. As they walked into the cool dimness of the villa he said, 'How have you entertained yourself without me?'

'I've swum a lot,' she said, forcing a light tone. 'And I've finished several books. You have a brilliant library here, and Maria assured me I could use it.'

'Of course. Have you done any exploring of the island?'

'I went with Maria into the market to buy fish; that was great fun, but apart from that and the swimming I've been disgustingly lazy.'

'Well-rested?' A glint in his eyes told her what he was insinuating.

Heat swept through her, sweet as honey, potent as wine. 'Very,' she said, falsely demure.

He laughed and took her hand, threading her fingers through his. 'We'd better go and eat lunch.' And as they walked into the cool house he added wickedly, 'First.'

Rosie's laughter was slightly forced, but it did help to ease her tension. All through lunch excitement built within her. The housekeeper had set the meal out on a small side terrace shaded by vines, the bunches of grapes already colouring up. A radiant sky glimmered through the leaves, its cobalt intensity matching the sweep of the sea, and the white sand sparkled.

'This is a wonderful place,' Rosie murmured as Gerd poured wine for her.

'It started off as a Roman villa,' Gerd told her, handing

her the glass. 'When that fell into decay the islanders sensibly used the stone for centuries to build and repair their own houses. Then in Victorian times sea bathing was thought to be health-giving, so one of my ancestors used the foundations to build this house for his delicate wife. And what do you think of our beaches?'

Rosie said blithely, 'Without conceding that New Zealand beaches—especially those around Kiwinui—can be beaten in any way, I have to admit that these are gorgeous.' Her eyes glinted as she shook her head. 'Although the island would be vastly improved by a screen of pohutukawa trees behind each beach.'

He laughed. 'You Kiwis! You're incorrigibly in love with your country.'

'Did the sea bathing help the delicate wife?'

He served her fish, cooked with sea salt and lemon slices. 'No, she died young.'

'That's sad.'

Gerd's smile was touched by cynicism. 'He mourned her for two years, and then married a robust and enthusiastic German princess who presented him with five healthy children. They all used to come here for their holidays. I believe it was an extremely happy marriage.'

She glanced at his face. Unreadable, as usual. Something tightened inside Rosie, warning her not to go in this direction. She knew what he wanted from her—an uncomplicated affair with no angst, nothing but shared passion. And a clean end to it when the time came.

Well, she could give him all of that.

With a theatrical sigh she attacked her fish. 'So much for a tragic love affair.'

'If they wanted to keep their integrity and their throne my ancestors had to be practical.'

Was he warning her not to develop any romantic hopes? She said, 'I hope the five children enjoyed their holidays here.'

'There are photographs showing that they did,' he told her.

The meal was superb; Maria used the foods of the island—fish, vegetables, olives and cheese and wine, pine nuts and basil—to produce magnificent, earthy dishes that echoed the Mediterranean.

Rosie watched in awe while Gerd ate with a healthy appetite, and was touched by Maria's delight when he demanded some of her yoghurt with honey and peaches at the end of the meal.

It was a pleasant return to the Gerd she remembered from those holidays in New Zealand when he'd just been Kelt's older brother and no one had thought anything of his position.

When she'd been a kid, and life had been simple.

'What are you thinking?' Gerd put down the spoon with which he'd demolished the dessert.

'About the holidays we used to have at Kiwinui,' she told him. 'And what fun they were. Remember when you decided to teach me how to ride?'

His smile was a little set. 'Indeed I do. You fell off every time you got onto the pony, but each time you picked yourself up, dusted yourself down and got onto her back with gritted teeth and determination.'

'She was a sweet-tempered little pony.'

'Do you still ride?'

'When I can.' The words sounded distant, and she

wished she hadn't started reminiscing. Her breath caught in her throat when he smiled at her.

As though he'd read her mind, Gerd picked up her hand from beside the plate and got to his feet, pulling her with him so that they faced each other.

'Has Maria managed to persuade you to take a siesta?' he asked, his voice deepening.

Rosie's heartbeat began to speed up erratically. 'She's tried, but I usually read.'

'A waste of a good siesta,' he stated autocratically, lashes drooping as he surveyed her face.

Quick excitement bubbled through her. 'Oh, really?' she said demurely. 'What other things can one do in siesta time? Besides sleeping, of course.'

'Things like this.'

Amusement fled, leaving behind only the passion, and she arched flagrantly into him as he bent his head and kissed her. All through lunch she'd been trying not to anticipate this moment. Now she surrendered to the erotic power of his mouth taking hers in a kiss so flagrantly sexual it robbed her of breath and set her pulses hammering heavily in her ears.

She felt herself being lifted and said dreamily, 'This is getting to be a habit.'

'A habit I enjoy,' he said, shouldering his way through a wide doorway.

'Because it makes you feel big and macho?'

His smile was a flash of white. 'Possibly because the only time I have some control over you is when your feet aren't on the floor.'

'I don't believe that. You deliberately changed my travel plans and lured me into abject surrender,' she drawled, folding one hand into a serviceable fist and hitting him firmly just above a rib.

'Ow!' she said when her fist met iron-hard resistance. She pulled back her hand and examined the reddened knuckles with rueful amusement.

'Never signal your intentions,' he said calmly. 'I had time to tighten the muscles.'

He must have chosen the room she was using, because even as she opened her mouth to tell him where it was he turned into the doorway. Strangely enough that gave her a warm feeling of being cared for.

Eyes glinting, he slid her down the length of his body, letting her feel just how she affected him, and by the time she was standing once more all sensible thought had fled and when she said his name it was in an urgent, harsh whisper.

'Yes,' he said, his voice raw and tense. 'But before—I assume you were prescribed contraception before you came down here?'

Some of her lovely anticipation leached away. 'Yes.'

'How long is it before it takes effect?'

She knew exactly. 'Another four days.'

He nodded, and kissed her with a lingering passion that rekindled the fire within. When he lifted his head his lashes were lowered so that all she could see beneath them was a line of gold.

'Then we know where we are,' he said thickly. 'We'll just have to be careful until then.'

Separation had honed their hunger to extremes; the first time they'd made love it had been slow and intensely sensuous, but now they fell onto the bed and came together with such a ferocious appetite that Rosie climaxed almost immediately, gasping something—Gerd's name, she realised later—in a sort of chant while sensation overwhelmed her in a maelstrom of passionate need.

Shuddering, clinging, she rode the storm wherever it took her. As she began to come down again she watched him, his handsome face stark and angular in the shuttered dimness, his head flung back and his eyes closed.

Minutes—hours?—later, he scooped her to lie across him in a tangle of limbs. 'There,' he drawled, his voice lazy and amused. 'Wasn't that better than reading? Or sleeping?'

Better than anything she'd ever experienced before...

But the words remained unspoken. He was keeping things very pragmatic, his uncompromising will containing that untamed passion so that he was always in control.

Well, she had to pretend to be just as cool, just as emotionally uninvolved.

'Mmm,' she murmured, withdrawing into herself.

'However, sleep has its place.' He tucked her head into his shoulder.

She had never felt so...safe, she thought dreamily as exhaustion claimed her.

But when she woke she was alone, and it was twilight.

No, she thought after a shaken glance at her watch, it was dawn! She'd slept the whole evening and night through. Shivering, she huddled under the light covering he must have put over her before he left and forced herself to look at the end of their affair.

They'd spend a month on this enchanted island

together—a month in which she'd fall further and further in love with Gerd—and at the end they'd say a civilised farewell. Then she'd return to New Zealand, and he'd go back to his palace and the real, important part of his life.

She should leave for New Zealand now, while she was still…what? Heart-whole?

A laugh that sounded too close to a sob broke from her. Her heart already belonged to Gerd.

No, it was more courageous to stay, to search for the real, fallible man behind the façade he presented to the world. Surely, discovering that he had faults and idiosyncrasies like every other man would replace the hero worship of her childhood and adolescence with a mature adult understanding?

Or was she just weak and needy, grasping at any straw so she could enjoy the only time she'd ever have with him?

'And if I am?' she said half out loud.

She'd never get what she wanted from Gerd. It was time to face that and accept it, however much it hurt.

Slowly she got up and walked across to the windows, adjusting the blades of the shutters so she could see the beach. The crystalline sand blinded her and she closed her eyes against it and turned away.

All her life she'd been in hiding. Few of those who knew her had any idea that her bright personality was a façade to shield the child who'd known herself unloved by her parents. Kelt, perhaps, understood—and possibly Hani…

These next four weeks were all she'd ever have of Gerd, so she'd show grace and courage and style; when she left him she wanted him to see her as a woman he could admire, as well as the lover he'd enjoyed physically.

Did she have the courage to do that—to love unreservedly, knowing she'd have to walk away from him without a backward glance?

She dragged in a ragged breath.

Yes. Loving him would give her the strength to say farewell—and mean it in both senses of the word. She wished him nothing but good in his future.

Surely, if she could do that, she'd be able to leave him behind emotionally as well as physically.

Because people did recover from shattered hearts and unrequited love. They picked themselves up and went on, and eventually they were happy again.

Mind made up, she got ready for a month of bittersweet joy.

The next couple of days passed in a haze of pleasure. As each golden evening slid into the passionate darkness of night Rosie discovered how happiness tasted, how it coloured her world, what a difference loving Gerd and knowing that he wanted her made. Most of the time she could ignore the nagging knowledge of future grief and gave herself over to pleasure, to a deep, intense delight in his presence that she'd never allowed herself before.

She'd never imagined a person could be so happy, she mused dreamily, waking up on the third morning. The only flaw was that so far she'd slept alone; Gerd made love to her and then left her.

In some way his refusal to share a bed with her seemed to symbolise the distance between them—a distance that not even their passion could bridge.

Once up she straightened her shoulders. No whining; she'd accept the bitter with the sweet. And nothing was sweeter than making love with Gerd...

A cool shower revived her and she had just dressed in shorts and a T-shirt when someone knocked on the bedroom door.

Excitement funnelled through her, catching her breath and imparting an extra radiance to her smile. 'Come in,' she called.

Her heart swelled when she saw him. 'Gerd—New Zealand style,' she teased, eyeing his long, tanned legs and the casual cotton shirt—although, knowing Gerd, she suspected both had been made to fit his rangy, lean body.

'I could say the same.' His smile tightened as he let his gaze roam from her sunny curls to her bare feet. 'In Regency England they'd have called you a pocket Venus, and a diamond of the first water.'

She gave a theatrical sigh and came towards him. 'Typical,' she said. 'Trust me to be born into a time when the fashion is for narrow hips and no waist.' She laughed up at him. 'How do you know so much about Regency England?'

'It's a period I find interesting—the infiltration of the old aristocracy by up-and-coming industrialists. Not many countries dealt with the resultant power shift so creatively as the British.'

She said thoughtfully, 'Does it have relevance for Carathia?'

'I think it does.' He changed the subject. 'Would you like to go sailing?'

'Now?'

He smiled down at her. 'Why not? There's food on the yacht—Maria has stocked it with enough to feed an army. Along the coast there's a bay with the ruins of a Greek temple to Aphrodite overlooking it. It's in remarkably good repair, probably because the Romans took it over, and then in the Christian era the islanders simply dedicated the temple to the Virgin.'

Intrigued, she asked, 'So it's a church now?'

'It was never used for actual worship—or not in modern times, anyway. Maria says that lovers still make pilgrimages to it with offerings of flowers in the hope that the goddess will guarantee them a happy romance.'

A sacrifice to love. Perhaps she should try that.

'I'd like to see it,' she told him.

He held out his hand. 'Come on, then.'

The yacht was quite small, easily handled by two. Remembering the burly man who'd ridden with them the night they went out to dinner, Rosie said, 'You obviously don't need security here.'

He gave her a keen glance, but his answer was delivered in a non-committal voice. 'Not here, no.'

'I'm glad,' she said, and then wished she hadn't said that. If Gerd realised how much she loved him he might call a halt to their relationship. So she added airily, 'I felt rude talking to you and ignoring both him and the chauffeur.'

'They wouldn't have been able to hear,' he said, loosening the mainsheet.

'I know, but although my mother is a stickler for manners she didn't actually instruct me in the correct way to treat bodyguards.'

'It's quite simple—you let them do their jobs without interference. Can you get my sunglasses? They're on a shelf in the saloon.'

Not particularly luxurious, the saloon sported a table beside the neat, efficient galley area, and some very comfortable seating. A door led to another cabin further forward that probably held a bed.

It intrigued her that Gerd, who'd forged a worldwide business before his thirtieth birthday, chose this yacht instead of something huge and opulent.

Handing the sunglasses over, she said as much, and he shrugged, donning them so she couldn't discern his expression.

'I enjoy sailing,' he said as though that explained everything.

Rosie decided his words and actions were explanation enough. Clearly he relished the physical effort of hauling on ropes and sails, and the mental contest with the wind and the waves around the rocky coastline.

'I can do that,' she said at one stage, scrambling to haul in a jib sheet after they went about.

He watched her pull it in until the sail stopped flapping. 'Thanks. Although you don't need to—it's set up for single-handed sailing.'

Which meant he sailed it by himself.

Or that the other women he brought here to visit the love goddess's temple weren't sailors, she thought realistically.

That hurt, but she ignored it. *Live for the moment* was her new mantra, and she intended to follow it without obsessing about what had gone before, or regretting what would come after.

Even though living for the moment meant living dangerously.

But she'd lived safely for years, and it had got her nothing but emptiness.

CHAPTER SIX

THE temple took Rosie's breath away. Still creamy-white after more than two thousand years on the headland, its perfect proportions and clean lines were as elegant as they had been when it was first built.

'It's—truly sublime,' she breathed.

Gerd gave a final tug to the anchor chain, and turned. She hadn't actually been talking to him; the words had come unconsciously. She was perched on the cockpit seat so that her legs were displayed to their best advantage, and a surge of lust gripped him so that he had to turn away to hide his physical response.

Although the top of her head barely reached his shoulder, she was strong; every cell in his body recalled the clamp of those legs around his hips, and he wanted her with a fierceness that clenched his hands by his sides. As elegantly curved as Aphrodite herself, her skin gleaming ivory-gold in the sunlight, she could have posed for a statue of the goddess.

Hell, he wanted to take her there and then. Perhaps the goddess was having a sly joke at his expense?

Leashing his unslaked appetite, he told her abruptly, 'They built her temple here because Aphrodite was born of the sea.'

Her upwards glance held a certain restraint that echoed in her tone. 'She's certainly got a great view of it from there. Can we climb up from the beach?'

'If you don't mind scrambling in the heat.'

'Will my shoes be suitable?'

Gerd checked her slender feet, sensibly enclosed in boat shoes. 'They'll be fine.'

The path wound up from the bay, steep but mostly shaded by the silvery leaves of ancient olives. Before they started Gerd said, 'If you think it will be too steep we can come here in the car one day.'

'No,' she said, looking amused. 'I'm sure I can cope, but if I can't then you can carry me. Although perhaps it would be a bit much to expect.'

He laughed, eyes gleaming as he said, 'If you can't get there I'll be more than happy to carry you.'

Her look sizzled with invitation, but she went on, 'I forgot to bring my camera, and I'd like to photograph this, so yes, it would be great to come again.'

And cope she did, scrambling up in front of him so that he was tormented by the sight of golden legs and the seductive sway of her hips.

'You're fit,' he observed.

She cast him a sly, laughing glance over her shoulder. 'So you don't need to stay behind me in case I fall or fade. My landlady has a dog—a fairly large mutt. Mrs Harley is elderly and although she takes him for a nice, gentle walk to the shops every day he needs more than that, so I do a morning and evening shift, and we walk up One Tree Hill and back down again.'

He recalled the extinct volcano, one of many that dotted Auckland. High and grass-covered, its terraced slopes revealing its past as a Maori fortress—it reared above the city, an excellent workout for both dog and handler.

Gerd asked casually, 'Do you ever think of leaving Auckland?'

She sent him a startled glance. 'If I had a good enough reason I would,' she said after a moment. 'Not that I dislike Auckland. I love Kiwinui. That's always been my ideal.'

Because Kelt lived there? The thought goaded Gerd into silence. Once at the top he watched as she turned to examine the building with wide, awed eyes, and answered her questions as best he could, intrigued by her quick curiosity and interest in everything.

Why had he asked her to come to his coronation? Oh, he'd told her it was because he saw her as family. It hadn't been exactly a lie—more a convenient half-truth.

Admitting that he felt there was unfinished business between them would have given her invitation too much importance.

She interrupted his reluctant admission by pointing towards a distant hillside village. 'I presume the grassed-over track from there used to be the route to the temple.'

'Yes, the ancient processional way. When we come by car I'll leave the vehicle in the village and we'll walk up that path.'

'I'm amazed it's still visible after all these centuries,' she said reflectively, her tone quiet and solemn.

'It was probably used quite regularly until fairly recently.'

'What are the bushes growing in that gully?'

Amusement tinged his words. 'Actually, a very distant relative of the pohutukawa that grows by your beaches. It's a myrtle and is sacred to Aphrodite. It's flowering now, in fact—they're creamy-white, and sweetly scented.'

An underlying note in his voice lifted the hair on the back of Rosie's neck. She didn't know how to deal with this, she thought despairingly. They weren't touching, but she was so aware of him her skin felt taut and stretched, as though he had the power to affect her physically from a distance.

It was too much—sensory overload. Turning abruptly, she gazed at the temple again, a monument to the power and strength of physical love, and thought how incredibly appropriate that was.

Did Gerd make a habit of bringing his lovers here...?

'Is it safe to explore inside?' she asked brightly, pushing the ugly query into the back of her mind and refusing to allow it to hurt.

'It's in good condition. There have been tactful repairs made these past few years.'

She cast him a swift look. 'Did you have anything to do with that?'

'I've set up a foundation to care for the ancient monuments of Carathia,' he said, and began to tell her of the statue that had been found near by, a magnificent thing of creamy Parian marble lost so long ago its existence had become a myth, only half-believed until it was found by a peasant in his olive grove. 'It had been buried so carefully that it was remarkably intact.'

'Where is it?' she asked, looking around the empty expanse of the temple.

'In a museum in the biggest town over on the mainland coast,' he told her, and answered the query in her glance. 'For security. It was almost stolen.'

She said, 'I suppose that's a constant fear.'

'It is,' he said grimly. 'There are extremely rich men who'd enjoy nothing more than to gloat over something as beautiful and rare.'

Rosie nodded. 'I've read about that, but to me it sounds sick.'

'You could say it shows a commendable love of beauty.'

'But you don't believe that,' she said swiftly.

'No.' The flat, lethal tone of his voice revealed more than his dispassionate words. 'Like you, I think it shows a sick desire to own something no one else can enjoy.' He gestured at a marble podium. 'She stood there.'

Rosie said, 'Oh—look.'

On the ancient stone someone had put flowers—a white-ribboned posy made up of the golden daisies that dotted the processional way and the fringed, delicately perfumed flowers that had to be myrtle.

'An offering,' Gerd told her. 'Someone wants something from the goddess.'

'Or is thanking her.'

'That possibly,' he agreed. 'Come and see the view from the front.'

It was astonishingly beautiful, a great spread of violet-blue sea dotted by islands, all overlooked by a sky as brilliant and clear. While the soft wind swirled and played amongst the golden flowers Gerd named each island,

and showed her the darkness to the north that was the mainland of Europe.

'Greece and Asia lie to the east,' he said, 'and Italy to the west.'

She said soberly, 'For some strange reason it makes me horribly homesick.'

He surveyed her quizzically. 'Both have sea,' he agreed, 'and an island shelters the Kiwinui coastline. Apart from that I don't see much resemblance. Kiwinui is lush and green, every gully thick with bush and flax, and it looks out on to thousands of miles of open ocean. And although the myrtle is a vague connection to pohutukawa, it really doesn't look like it.'

'I think that's the problem—it's so completely different.' She gave an ironic smile and shrugged. 'But this is glorious. I can see why you like to come here for holidays.'

He took her hand and laced her fingers in his, his eyes direct and cool and too perceptive. 'I think you need something to drink. We'll go back to the boat and have lunch.'

'Thank you,' she said automatically, her breath catching in her throat as she met his eyes. Anticipation heated her blood, and she looked away again, feeling the slow pulse of desire throb through her body.

On the yacht he insisted on organising the meal, moving deftly around the area that served as a kitchen, and while she drank the glass of champagne he'd given her he downed a beer, and told her stories of the island that made her laugh and occasionally sigh.

After lunch he waited until she drained the coffee he'd

made for her before asking, 'Do you want to go ashore again?'

'I—no,' she said quietly.

'Good, because I don't either,' he said, and bent his head and kissed the place where her neck and shoulder met.

His lips were warm and seeking, and slow, hungry tremors coursed through her when he bit the skin there lightly. Rosie made an inarticulate little noise and turned her head into his shoulder.

'What is it?' His voice was harsh.

She looked up and saw passion darken his eyes, but although he wanted her she knew it wasn't in the all-consuming way she longed for him. 'Nothing,' she whispered.

And yielded to his practised caresses and her own urgent passion. This time it was languid, yet intense; he kissed her with his desire held well in check until she was gasping and aching, her body on fire and her voice gone.

The other cabin did contain a bed, and there, rocked by the tiny wavelets, they reached the agonised rapture of delight.

This time the climax was so sweet and prolonged Rosie had to close her eyes to hide the tears, but perhaps he noticed. As she started the slow downwards glide he began again, driving her mercilessly on into an ecstasy that left her shaking and mindless, her whole world narrowed to this man, to Gerd, to this moment in his arms, linked to him in the only way he would allow.

And when they finally slid into sleep, he was still with her, still keeping everything but joy at bay.

When she woke she was still in his grip, her body moulded to his, the regular rise and fall of his chest telling her he hadn't wakened.

This was the first time he'd stayed with her, the first—and probably the only—time she'd ever wake in his arms...

Forcing up heavy eyelids, she took the rare chance to scan his beloved face without the fear of him catching her at it. Such perfect features, she thought, eyeing the arrogant blade of his nose, his strong jaw, the masculine beauty and strength that was his mouth...

Memories of what his mouth could do to her made her shiver deliciously.

Silently she adored his skin's golden sheen, the long, powerful lines of his body—the body that could take her on an erotic journey to paradise, that rapturous nirvana where her very sense of self was cut loose and she could only surrender to the dark enchantment of Gerd's magnetism.

Her heart started to pick up speed and her breasts bloomed, the nipples tight buds of excitement—waiting for his mouth, for his touch...

Without thinking she stretched out tentative fingers and skimmed his flat, muscled midriff, only to snatch back her hand at his movement. She froze, but almost immediately he sank back into sleep.

Slowly her gaze drifted down, past lean hips...

Her breath came faster when she realised he was aroused. Heat smouldered into life within her, moistening the passage that longed for him, contracting internal muscles she'd barely learned how to use.

Barely able to breathe in a mixture of shyness and

reckless hunger, she touched him, her fingers lingering as she explored. Silky and hot, yet hard and—getting harder, she realised.

She glanced up, but his eyes were still closed, and she realised that, although his breathing had quickened, he was still asleep.

Curious, excited, she tightened her hand gently around him.

He moved like lightning, so quickly she only had time to gasp when he plunged into her, his big, lithe body taut as a bowstring. Drowning in erotic pleasure, Rosie arched against him, and he flung his head back and spilled into her as she climaxed around him, her body taut and seeking, her heart thundering wildly in her breast.

Gerd said something—her name—and then swore violently in Carathian, his face dark with anger as he tore himself free from her to sit on the edge of the bed, his spine dead straight and the broad, glistening shoulders set.

Still shaking from the elemental passion of that urgent coupling, Rosie sat up too, pushing her wet curls back from her face, shocked at the swift ferocity of their joining. She looked up at his back, so squarely presented to her, and closed her eyes at the red marks her fingernails had clawed across the broad expanse.

'Oh, *God*,' she whispered, appalled. 'We just made love—'

He got to his feet and turned, towering over the bed like some grim deity from ancient times. 'We did,' he agreed, his voice lethal. 'With no protection. How long does it take for the Pill to work?'

'Seven days,' she said in a muted voice.

'So we're not quite in the safe zone yet?' he asked on a note that brought her head up with a jerk.

We, he'd said. The automatic coupling of them as a unit gave her a little comfort.

'No,' she said, and her breath clogged her throat as she remembered—too late—that he'd knocked on her door before she'd taken one of the tablets she'd been religiously swallowing these past few mornings.

'What is it?' he demanded, his eyes suddenly intent.

Sickly, she told him. 'I didn't even think of it,' she whispered.

Because she'd been spellbound by the prospect of a whole day alone with him. 'Gerd, I'm so sorry.' Her voice shook and she couldn't say any more.

She didn't know what to expect. Anything—accusation, denunciation, ordinary old fury—would be appropriate, she thought half-hysterically.

After one glance at his face she looked away. The angular features were stark and honed, formidable, but, oddly enough, not angry. He probably looked like this when he was faced with a constitutional problem.

Her breath hurt in her starved lungs when she took a rapid breath.

In a voice so aloof it made her shiver, he said, 'Do you have the tablets with you?'

'No,' she said miserably. 'They're in the bathroom at the villa.' She hadn't gone back in there after he'd come for her, and she hadn't thought of taking one because she was so ridiculously, *stupidly* happy at the prospect of a whole day with him...

'So there's a reasonably good chance that you're completely unprotected.'

'I don't know, but there's a warning about using other protection if you miss one...' Her voice trailed away as he stood up and walked across to the porthole, staring out as though—as though he couldn't bear to look at her.

Then and there, Rosie made up her mind that if she was pregnant she would love their baby enough for two.

'It's just five days since I took the first one,' she said bleakly. 'I didn't—I didn't know that—'

'You didn't realise men could make love while they were asleep,' he said in a level voice that told her nothing.

She pushed her wildly curling hair back from her hot face. His earlier words echoed in her mind like doom-bringers. *No protection.*

'No,' she admitted in a muted voice.

'So now you do know. Anyway, it wasn't your fault.'

But it was. She'd touched him, caressed him...

He said, 'There is something—the morning-after Pill.'

No!

Appalled, she gazed at his arrogant features, so controlled she couldn't read anything but an inflexible decisiveness when he went on harshly, 'I would prefer not to go that way, but I realise the decision is yours to make.'

'I don't...I know it seems silly, but I can't help but feel it's...' Rosie floundered, then said on a jagged indrawn breath, 'I don't want to do that. Do your pharmacies here sell test kits?'

'I'll get one sent from the capital,' he said curtly. 'It will be more discreet.'

'I'm so sorry.'

'Why?' He gave her a tight smile. 'For giving me the best sex I've ever had?'

Pink-cheeked, she accused, 'You said you were asleep!'

'Not for long,' he said drily, his face relaxing as he surveyed her. 'But I could no more have stopped than I can fly. We'd better get dressed.'

Once back at the villa he said, 'Go and take that pill now.'

Heart sinking, she hurried inside and swallowed the wretched thing, closing her eyes to the warning on the packet. For long seconds she stood in the bathroom, one hand pressed to her heart, and then she straightened her shoulders and walked back to help Gerd tidy the yacht. While he coiled ropes she made the bed, biting her lip when all evidence of their wild mating had been erased.

They walked back together, tension tightening between them like invisible cords.

Keep it light, she warned herself. But no, her wilful heart had to wildly complicate an already tangled situation. And now this...

He broke into her sombre thoughts. 'Would you like to go out to dinner?'

No, she wanted to go into her bedroom and howl like a banshee. Instead, she nodded and said sedately, 'That would be lovely, thank you.'

But that night they didn't make love. Rosie understood; she too didn't want to risk anything until she knew the result of her madness. Yet she found herself dreaming of babies, of losing something precious and irretrievable, waking a couple of times in the darkness with tears running down her cheeks.

The parcel from the pharmacist was scheduled to arrive after lunch the next day—a day with a sullen sun behind a bank of cloud, followed by rain scudding in across the sea.

Over a late breakfast Gerd said, 'I have papers to deal with. Will you be all right?'

Rosie lifted her brows. 'Of course I will,' she said solemnly. 'I need to give myself a manicure.'

'And that will take all morning?'

Rosie smiled. 'No,' she admitted. 'Gerd, don't worry about me—I'm able to entertain myself.'

To her surprise he picked up her hands and examined them. 'They look perfect as they are,' he said, adding with a narrow smile, 'and on my skin they feel... exquisite. And so very creative.'

He laughed at the fiery colour across her cheekbones, and carried her hands to his mouth, kissing each palm. 'I hope you don't plan to paint your nails black.'

'Black doesn't suit me,' she said promptly. Her need for him was a sharp pain, and his kisses sent the familiar quiver of delight through her. She went on, 'Besides, my mother always says that when you're on holiday clear polish is the only appropriate shade.'

In the end she did give herself a manicure. She'd just reassured herself that the polish had dried when her cellphone rang.

Startled, she lifted it. 'Hello?'

As though her words that morning had conjured her mother, Eva said tartly, 'You might have let me know where you were.'

'You have my number.' What had caused this unusual call?

'Yes, well, I've been busy, and there's been no need.' Eva paused to give weight to her next words. 'Until I picked up the paper this morning. Do you realise you're all over the newspapers of most of the world?'

'*What?*'

'You heard,' Eva told her. 'Surely you didn't think you could go off with Gerd and not have the paparazzi come along too? They've been waiting with bated breath for him to announce his engagement to Princess Serina, so photos of you together are particularly juicy.'

Rosie realised she was shaking, her fingers clenched around the telephone. 'But there haven't been any photographers—'

'Oh, yes, there have,' her mother interrupted. 'At least one's got a photo of you gazing dreamily up at Gerd—and sold it to every newspaper in New Zealand, it seems. According to a friend in London, the papers there are on to it too. Oh, they're careful to say you're a cousin of Gerd's, but that photo is pretty damning.'

Sick apprehension chilled Rosie. 'Damn,' she whispered.

Her mother said acidly, 'I hope you're not pinning any hopes on marrying him.'

'Of course I'm not.'

'Well, that's something, I suppose.' Eva paused, but when Rosie didn't speak she went on in irritation, 'Honestly, Rosemary, what are you *thinking*? I know you've always had a yen for him, but he's more or less engaged to that princess, and she's not going to be happy that he's spending a dirty week with you before their betrothal goes official.'

Rosie bit her lip. She wasn't going to tell her mother that Gerd had promised her there was no relationship between him and the oh-so-suitable princess. 'Thanks for telling me,' she said levelly. 'I'd better go now.'

And let Gerd know. She felt sick, besmirched as she left the room to do just that. But she met him halfway to the room he called the study and realised he'd already found out. His brows were drawn together in a forbidding frown, and his beautiful mouth was a thin, straight line.

When she opened her mouth he held up a hand. 'We need to talk.'

'My mother's just rung,' she said quietly.

His face darkened further. 'What did she have to say?'

Briefly she enlightened him.

He bit off words in Carathian, and said, 'I've heard from my chief minister.'

'Is it so bad? I mean—you've had relationships before and you're not...'

Her voice trailed away as her mother's words echoed in her ears. *Just been about to announce his engagement...*

Had he lied to her? No, she thought, torn by anger and despair. Surely not.

Not Gerd.

But he said curtly, 'There's more to this than headlines.' He looked around the wide hall. 'Come into the study; it's going to take some explaining.'

In his office—a large room, half-office, half-sitting

room, with a massive sofa in front of a fireplace at one end—he showed her the photograph on his computer screen. Frowning, she peered at it.

Clearly taken from some distance with a telephoto lens, it showed her and Gerd standing together. He had his arm around her shoulders, and she was laughing up at him. Thank heavens her shorts and shirt were discreet and not at all sexy, she thought, relieved for a second until that sick apprehension kicked back in.

Because she was looking at Gerd with her heart in her eyes.

'Where—? Oh, of course,' she said, realising it had been taken at the temple of Aphrodite.

'He—or she—must have been in the clump of trees on the next headland,' Gerd said without inflection.

Biting her lip, she straightened up. 'It's not too bad. I mean, I'm just laughing, and that's just a casual hug...' Her voice trailed away.

His brows lifted. 'No one looking at that could fail to see that we're lovers.'

Rosie took a deep breath. We *are* lovers, he'd said. Well, it was true—or had been until she'd lost her head on the yacht.

'All right, but I'm still missing something here. Why is this a disaster?'

'It's not a disaster,' he returned, so coolly detached she could have hit him. 'It's a complication. Come and sit down.'

Once on that wide sofa, she looked at him, her heart clamping. He leaned against the stones of the fireplace and said without preamble, 'Do you know anything about Carathia's legend of the second son?'

'Yes.' Astonished, she stared at him. What on earth had an ancient legend got to do with that photograph? 'Well, not much, really, only enough to know that there is a legend that caused you problems. It surfaced when your grandmother confirmed you as her heir—some idiots wanted Kelt instead because the legend says that if there are disasters and hardship it's because the wrong son is ruling the country, and the only thing to do is depose the current Grand Duke and put his sibling on the throne.'

His mouth thinned. 'And several hundred people died because of it.'

Rosie nodded. 'Yes, I remember. It was horrible, but what does it have to do with us?'

'Bear with me,' he told her austerely. 'A thousand years ago Carathia was ruled by my ancestor.'

'The Greek mercenary—the one who saved Carathia from being overrun?'

He shook his head. 'No, the Norseman who arrived here via Russia. His oldest son inherited the throne; unfortunately for him plague struck, and then they were invaded by a horde from Asia. They were still fighting them off when this area was hit by a tidal wave caused by an earthquake in the eastern Mediterranean. The ruler was deemed unlucky, and the people rebelled, forcing him from the throne and installing his younger brother in his place.'

'And that's what this legend is based on?'

'Not entirely. As soon as the brother ascended the throne the horde withdrew, the plague died away and no further tidal waves have ever hit this coast. However, after his death the son who ascended to the throne had to face another war.'

'So they got rid of him and installed his younger brother?' Rosie guessed.

'Exactly. Who fought a triumphant war against the invaders and beat them decisively, and had a long and glorious reign. That's when the legend took root, mainly amongst the people in the mountains, who'd suffered greatly from war and plague. As you can imagine, this has caused endless turmoil down through the centuries; only rulers with no siblings felt safe on the throne. Even my grandmother had to fight a rebellion fomented by her younger sister.'

'Is that why Kelt's always lived in New Zealand?'

He looked at her almost approvingly. 'Yes. Of course, he's a born and bred Kiwi, and the last thing he wants is to rule Carathia.'

'So that's all right, then.' But it wasn't, she could tell from his expression. He looked—forbidding. 'I don't see what any of this has to do with me.'

With us...

Except that there was no *us*.

'Ever since then there has been a considerable amount of pressure on me to marry and provide heirs for the throne. I've been advised that it's probably the best way to make sure of a peaceful reign.'

Rosie fought to breathe, to be able to speak sensibly. She looked out of the window and realised that while she'd been in the study the clouds had been whisked away and the sun was shining outside. It seemed cruelly fateful.

'Go on,' Rosie said, bracing herself. He was going to tell her he'd lied, that he planned to marry the princess and produce those heirs to satisfy his people.

His smile was humourless. 'Those photographs have caused a furore in Carathia. No, they haven't been published there, but people have seen them on television beamed in from the surrounding countries.'

'But—you've had—I mean, there have been other relationships,' she said uncertainly. Nothing about the princess, but her relief was brief and followed by even more doubt.

He shrugged. 'Carathians are conservative—they didn't see my other women as fit candidates for Grand Duchess.'

And neither was she. Rosie's emotions see-sawed again into bitter darkness.

It had to be the princess...

'I'll leave Carathia today, then—that should stop any gossip.' Intent only on getting out of there with some pitiful scraps of pride intact, she got to her feet.

Ignoring her statement, he said uncompromisingly, 'The situation is complicated by the fact that you and I are connected, if not directly related. The Carathians have a history of cousin marriage.'

'But we're not really cousins!' She stopped, because something wasn't right. Searching his face, she could discern nothing beyond a formidably inflexible determination.

Uncertainly she said, 'Gerd, exactly what is this all about?'

Still showing no emotion, he said, 'I'm asking you to marry me.' His mouth twisted into something that could have been cynical amusement, but his gaze never left her face. 'Unfortunately, I'm making a complete and total hash of it.'

CHAPTER SEVEN

STUNNED, Rosie stared at Gerd's angular face, now expressionless and uncompromising. His predatory stillness shocked and alarmed her. She sensed an inevitable fate closing around her, something she both longed for and dreaded.

When she answered her voice trembled with both fear and an undercurrent of shameful yearning. 'Why?'

His eyes narrowed. 'You can ask that after what's happened between us?'

She longed for some indication of how he felt, of why he was doing this. Instead, in his handsome features she could read only a ruthlessness that cut her more severely than any knife ever could.

So painful to have her every hope answered in this way—to see her most ardent desire within reach and know she didn't dare accept it.

'Would it be so hard, Rosemary?' he asked, and came towards her.

'Don't you dare,' she choked.

'Don't dare what? Don't dare to touch you? When I know how much you like it?'

His voice was controlled, yet beneath the cool, almost ironic tone she heard another note—raw and elemental.

Nerves twanging, she stared at him, defying him without words.

Although a smile curved his beautiful mouth it didn't temper the unyielding intention Rosie sensed in him. Coldly deliberate, he was using the searing attraction that scorched the air between them to persuade her into surrender.

'When we both know how much you like *this*,' he emphasised, not taking that final step between them. Instead he reached out and traced the outline of her lips with a sensuous forefinger, so gently she hardly felt his touch.

That was all. His hand dropped to his side and he said, 'Rosemary.'

Just one word, but he didn't need to say anything more. That faint, intensely evocative scent that was his alone— the essential essence of the man—teased her nostrils.

He was aroused—as aroused as she was. The hunger he summoned so easily throbbed through her, eroding her determination, her knowledge that what he was proposing—and how cynical that was!—could only lead to anguish and grief.

Although every instinct urged her to get the hell out of there, she stayed, head high and her lips held in such a firm line they no longer trembled. At all costs she had to appeal to his icily rational brain before he kissed her. Once he did that she'd be lost.

If only Gerd hadn't been so honest—the honesty she'd demanded of him, she reminded herself savagely.

If he'd not told her of his position—the need for a wife, for children—she'd probably have been weak enough to agree to marry him. She loved him so much...

Dry-mouthed, hoping he couldn't see the naked

longing behind the screen of her lashes, she said bitterly, 'What we have is just sex—not a sensible basis for marriage.'

'*Just* sex?' The mocking note in his voice made her flush furiously, but before she could answer he went on more grimly, 'There is also the fact that by joining you here I have tarnished your reputation.'

'Oh, that's so old-fashioned.' She shivered at the sound of her heart cracking. 'Besides, being your lover should only enhance my reputation.'

'Amongst a certain sort of person,' he agreed with distaste.

Desperately Rosie surged on. 'Anyway, I don't have a reputation to tarnish—you were shocked when you discovered—' She jerked to a stop, disconcerted by the sudden glint in his eyes.

'That you were a virgin?' he supplied smoothly. 'Yes, startled, certainly—but delighted.'

'Why? Because it made me more *suitable*?'

She realised the instant she spoke that she should have stayed silent. Marriage had been the last thing on his mind when they'd made love at the palace!

Before he could answer she blurted, 'I'm not going to marry you because we've been lovers, or for reasons of state.' Beads of sweat gathered at her temples.

'Then how about the fact that you might be carrying my child?' he told her brusquely.

Cornered, she stared at his implacable face. How could she love him so—so violently, yet be so angry with him?

Steadying her breathing and her voice with an effort that clenched her fists, she said, 'You don't need to worry about that. No woman nowadays has to have a child they don't want.'

He didn't move, but she sensed a reaction so intense she took an involuntary step backwards.

'Is that what you would do?' His voice was level and without emotion.

Rosie couldn't lie to him. 'I—no,' she admitted wearily. 'But—however great your need for an heir, you don't have to go to the extreme of marrying me.'

'I will not turn my back on my child,' he said with icy precision. 'Or you.'

Oh, that tempted her—and hurt. Rosie unclenched her hands long enough to spread them out in front of her. 'Gerd, we don't know yet—'

'I would also prefer not to have the world know if my child was conceived out of wedlock.'

'Would it matter so much?' The words tumbled out before she realised what she'd said. She couldn't let him believe she was even considering any possibility of marriage, but before she had a chance to qualify her statement he spoke.

'Not to me personally, but it would to quite a large number of Carathians. They are a religious, moral people, and rather proud of being so.'

'Then they shouldn't try to force you to do things you don't want to.' Like marrying someone entirely unsuitable. Hurriedly, she added, 'If I am pregnant I'll go back to New Zealand and no one will ever know who the father is.' Another thought struck her. 'And...you wouldn't be turning your back on the—on any child because I'd agree to access whenever you wanted.'

'Don't be an idiot,' he said stonily. 'Rosemary, if there

is a child I want it to be an essential part of my life, not kept hidden away in New Zealand like a guilty secret. And you too—you deserve much more than that.'

She could have wept at that. He was being so intransigent—and for all the right reasons except the most important of all. 'You should marry Princess Serina—or someone like her. That way you'd satisfy your people and have a wife who knows how to behave as a Grand Duchess should.'

'I don't *want* to marry Serina.' The arrogant tone didn't abate at all when he added, 'And I imagine she'd be appalled if I asked her.'

Perhaps Serina had realised he didn't love her.

Rosie sternly quenched a foolish, irresponsible hope. That didn't mean he loved anyone else. He'd been forced into this position, and, being a man of honour he was determined to do his best for her and his possible baby.

His expression relaxed. 'I realise this has come as a shock to you,' he said more temperately. 'However, it is something I have been thinking about ever since you came here.'

Was there the slightest hesitation before the second half of that sentence, as though he'd substituted 'since you came here' for something else—something like 'since we made love without protection'?

'Why?' she asked baldly.

His smile was a masterful blend of irony and ruthless charm. 'You know the reason,' he said, his tone sending tiny, sensuous shivers through her. 'It has been there ever since we kissed three years ago.'

If only he would let her see his true emotions—but Rosie could read nothing in his face. She said tautly,

'I'm not going to agree to marry you because you need a wife and an heir to ratify your position, or because your people would be shocked if the baby was conceived out of wedlock.'

'Then how about because you want me?'

Her breath locked in her throat. 'Wanting's easy.' She tried to speak scathingly—boldly—but it came out sounding sorrowful. 'And commonplace,' she added, hoping the sting in her words would repel him.

'I forget that you know very little about sex and desire,' he observed. 'One of these days you must tell me why you were such an obstinate virgin. But trust me, Rosemary, that what we share is neither easy nor commonplace. Such communion is a rare treasure, one I've never experienced before, and one I'm reluctant to give up. Especially since there is no reason for such a vain sacrifice.'

White-faced, she watched him advance towards her, his intention plain.

How long could she hold out if he touched her—if he kissed her?

She stepped back, holding up her hands in a useless attempt to keep him away. He smiled, and bent his head and kissed her mouth.

One lonely night had sharpened her hunger into a craving that corroded her precarious self-control. Although Rosie fought the weakness, the promise of his kiss smashed down her fragile barricades in a surge of sensory overload of such intense sweetness she could no longer resist.

His arms came around her as she kissed him back, and he lifted his head to say against her lips, 'There's no need for such determined resistance, my sweet one. I will be a good husband to you.'

Rosie had no doubt of that. He'd be an ideal husband in every respect except one. On a half-sob she said, 'I wonder if this is how my mother feels every time she takes a new lover?'

His eyes narrowed. 'I don't think so,' he said, his voice cool. 'I doubt if she ever put up such a determined resistance to any man. And what she seeks from her lovers—unconditional love—is not to be found anywhere amongst humankind.'

Even as she accepted the validity of his logic, Rosie closed her eyes against it. Perhaps she was more like her mother than she'd realised.

Numbly she said, 'All right, if there's a baby I'll marry you.'

'You will marry me whether or not there is a child,' he stated, and at last kissed her properly, his arms closing around her as he carried her across to the big sofa.

And it wasn't one-sided; Rosie felt his body harden against her and shivered, exultant because he wanted her as much as she wanted him. Their mouths met again with such passion she felt herself melt, unable to think—unable to do anything but feel and want.

Against her lips Gerd muttered something before saying starkly, 'I need you. Here. Now.'

His raw tone shattered the last shards of her resistance. 'Yes,' she breathed into his ear, and found the opening of his shirt.

She ran a finger down it, relishing the smooth grain of his skin, the soft abrasion of the hair there. She knew exactly the pattern of that hair, the way it scrolled from one side of his chest to the other before arrowing down to disappear beneath his belt. She had followed that arrow...

Excitement pumped hot blood through her, a fierce sexual drive that transformed her into another person, a woman wanton with love, with desire.

She said harshly, 'I hope you have protection here.'

Eyes glittering, he rasped, 'I now have protection in every damned room in this villa.'

The muscles in his lithe body flexed with fluid power when he lifted her for another kiss. It felt like a brand, she thought dazedly, a seal on a contract...

It felt like heaven.

He set her down on the vast sofa, smoothly removing her T-shirt so that she was left in only her bra and trousers.

Her breasts tightened, and his eyes narrowed even further. 'I like that you can't hide your reaction to me,' he said. 'It makes me feel just a little less obvious.'

She expected him to take off the bra, a silky slither of flesh-coloured fabric. Instead he dropped to his knees beside the sofa and kissed her throat, then bent and took an importunate nipple into the moist heat of his mouth.

Instant fire. Instant, mindless need.

Desire so untrammelled the first waves of response shuddered through her. The pressure of his hand at the junction of her legs jerked her hips from the sofa in a thrust of animal hunger.

Gerd surveyed her, sprawled in helpless, voluptuous abandon before him. His face was drawn, set in lines of hunger and need that resonated shockingly through her as he took off her remaining clothes, making the process a drawn-out seduction that eventually had her almost sobbing in a potent mix of frustration and unfulfilled appetite.

But he stood and wrenched off his own clothes as though he couldn't bear to wait, and when they came together he fuelled that desperate pleasure, goading her further and further towards ecstasy until every muscle in her body screamed for release, for the ultimate passionate fulfilment that his big body and his consummate expertise would give her.

It came in an overwhelming wave of sensation that shook her heart, resounded in every cell, marked her for life. She was still buffeted by passion when Gerd reached his climax, head flung back as he poured himself into her. Locked in his arms, Rosie looked into the future and accepted a bitter truth she'd been afraid to face.

She'd learned to love Gerd when she was barely more than a child, and no other man would be able to take his place.

If she refused to marry him there would be no husband for her, no children...

Oh, she could make a good life, a worthwhile, even satisfying life, but there'd always be an emptiness at its core.

Tears gathered, an ache behind her eyes, and clogged her throat as she fought temptation. Why not stop yearning for the moon?

Why not marry him, take what joy she could from living with him and bearing his children?

Because it would kill something in her to know he didn't love her—would *never* love her the way she loved him. She only had to think of her mother, dedicating her life to a rash, fruitless search for that unconditional love Gerd had been so scathing about.

But there would be compensations, the siren voice whispered. And didn't the alternative seem bleak and unsatisfying?

Oh, yes, her heart mourned. Standing firm sounded staunch and positive, as did walking gallantly into a future without him. But when she thought of watching from a distance while he married someone else and sired those children his people needed...

Gerd stirred and said thoughtfully, 'I'm too big for this sort of thing.'

On an unwilling snort of laughter, she let herself be pulled up into his arms as he rose.

'If you're planning to make a habit of this, perhaps you should buy larger sofas,' she murmured.

He knew, she realised. Those hawk eyes saw too much, understood her too well.

'So, what is your decision?' His words were as uncompromising as his expression.

'I thought you'd already made it for me,' she returned acidly.

He shrugged. 'I hoped you'd see sense. But if not...' His gaze fell to her mouth, then moved to the soft mounds of her breasts. Amused yet relentless, he finished, 'If not, you have given me the perfect weapons to use against you.'

'Why are you pushing for this now—why not wait until after we know whether there is a baby or not?'

He said calmly, 'Because you would always feel that it was the child who caused my decision, and that is too great a burden for any child—and any marriage—to bear.'

If only he weren't so—honourable. And so right...

She said through her teeth, 'Tell me one thing—why do you think I'd make you a suitable wife?'

His mouth curving in an ironic smile, he said, 'I don't like the word suitable, but just this once I'll use your term. I know you, Rosemary. You're tough and vulnerable, straightforward and outgoing and intelligent and compassionate, and you make love like a very sexy angel. I've seen you with Kelt and Hani's little boy, and I like what I've seen. And I know you want me. I think together we can make a satisfying life and bring up happy children.'

Rosie felt his frankness like a blow to the heart. He didn't love her, and he wasn't trying to pretend that he did.

She said quietly, 'Thank you, but what makes you think that marrying you would be good for me?'

'I wonder if any other man in this world has to undergo such a catechism when he asks a woman to marry him.' He went on with formidable assurance, 'You will marry me, sweet girl. Because you want to. And because you know I want you to.'

And there, she thought wearily, he had her, because her love gripped her like a vice, locking her into a desperation so intense she could taste it.

With the heat of burning bridges on her back, she said starkly, 'All right, I'll marry you, but on one condition—two, actually.'

His face was unreadable. 'So—tell me these conditions.'

'That you're faithful.' How would he take this? She angled her chin at him and met his steady dark gaze without flinching, determined to make him understand. 'And that you'll always continue to be honest with me.'

'Of course.' He held her eyes, his own keen and searching. 'And I ask the same of you.'

'Yes,' she said simply.

Because too many emotions were roiling inside her, threatening to erupt in wildly humiliating disarray, she looked down at the clothes scattered on the floor and started to laugh.

A disconcerting note too close to hysteria alarmed her into abrupt silence. 'We'd better get dressed,' she managed to say, relieved when her voice sounded normal.

A distant clatter made her gasp and fling herself off the sofa, sheer terror clutching at her as she hauled on her clothes, gabbling, 'That must be—but it's too soon—it's not—'

'Calm down,' he said quietly. And when she went white, he held her shoulders and said, 'Don't look so horrified. Whatever happens now, I will be with you and beside you.'

Half an hour later she came out of her bathroom, to find him standing inside her bedroom door, his face expressionless.

'I'm not pregnant. The test kit showed a negative,' she said tonelessly, 'so we don't need to—'

'Stop right there,' Gerd said between his teeth. 'You made me a promise.'

'But there's no need to go on with it now,' she cried, hiding her misery with a show of anger.

'It's too late,' he said. 'I've already contacted my Press

secretary, and he's alerted the media for an announcement later today. I've drafted one out, but I need you to verify a few facts.'

Rosie stared at him incredulously, fighting back rage and a horrible feeling of helplessness. 'Why have you done this?'

'Because I suspected that if you weren't presented with a fait accompli you'd waste a considerable amount of time trying to persuade me to change my mind.'

His look should have put her in her place, but she was too angry to be subdued by any intimidating and utterly infuriating air of authority.

Hands clenching at her sides, she fought for words, finally coming up with an inane, 'You had no *right* to go ahead.'

'You agreed to marry me,' he said dispassionately. 'Naturally I warned my secretary, as it will be his job to deal with the media.'

'But—so soon...' Her voice trailed away, because of course she knew why he'd done it—to stop any further restlessness amongst his people.

From now on her life would be dedicated to Carathia, its welfare paramount. Rosie realised that secretly she'd hoped—oh, for a miracle, for Gerd to put her first.

It wasn't going to happen.

His voice cool, he asked, 'Why should we delay? By now probably everyone in Carathia knows you are here with me, so it is better that they realise who you are and why you are here.'

She could think of nothing to say that. After a few seconds she said, 'I'd better ring my mother, I suppose.'

'I have just rung her,' he said smoothly. 'Kelt and Hani

also, and of course Alex. None of them seemed surprised. They all send their love and best wishes. Your mother will arrive in two days' time.' He waited for a couple of beats, then added too blandly, 'On her own.'

Thank heaven for that. Rosie asked, 'Is she coming here?'

For some reason she didn't want her mother in this lovely place where for such a short time she'd been so happy.

'We'll meet her in the capital.' He gave her a keen, too-perceptive glance and said, 'You haven't had lunch, Rosemary, and Maria is cross with us for not letting her know ahead of time so that she could prepare something special.'

She put aside her shocking, unexpected grief when she'd gazed at the pregnancy indicator and realised she wasn't carrying Gerd's baby. 'We'd better go and eat whatever she has prepared. But in future you should remember that I don't like surprises.'

His brows drew together. 'Then I shall endeavour not to present you with any more. Come now, and as there is no child you can drink some of the champagne I've chosen.'

Although Maria might have been cross, not a sign of it showed. Beaming at them both, she launched into a stream of rapid Carathian, pausing only long enough for Gerd to translate, 'She is wishing us a long and happy life with many brave, handsome sons and beautiful daughters.'

Rosie pulled herself together to smile, to assume what she hoped was the happy air of a newly betrothed woman. 'Thank her, and tell her I'm not so sure about *many* sons, but if the ones we have are as brave and handsome as you I'll be content.'

And was surprised to see a tinge of colour along his arrogant cheekbones as he relayed this to the housekeeper, who laughed and bustled away, still chuckling. He pulled out a chair for her, and waited until she sat down.

'I didn't expect you to go ahead and announce everything without talking to me about it,' she said quietly.

He sat down, the sunlight sifting through the flowers to give his black hair a dark ruby sheen. The warm light played over his classic Mediterranean features, their beauty reinforced by uncompromising strength. Eyes so close to gold shouldn't be cold, but Gerd's were right then.

Rosie's heart clamped painfully. *What had she done?*

Too late now to ask herself that question. She'd made a decision and now she had plenty of time—all her life—to repent it.

Or make the most of it…

A note of exasperation coloured his voice. 'I am sorry if the speed of the announcement bothers you. Perhaps I should have offered you time to become accustomed to the idea of marrying me, but I thought you understood that we might not have that luxury.'

Well, she'd left herself open to that. Biting her lip, Rosie nodded. He *had* made it plain. And she had agreed.

It was time to stop behaving like someone who wanted to be loved. If she kept this up he might suspect that she was longing—*aching*—for his love, and pride was all she had now.

'I did.' Her voice trembled a little, and she had to take a breath to steady it before she could go on. 'I didn't realise that a day or so would make any difference.'

'It might not have,' he admitted, pouring two glasses of champagne.

He'd seen her in so many ways—exquisite in her ball-dress, elegant in the softly pastel silk suit she'd worn to his coronation, casual in shorts and a suntop on the yacht.

Naked in his arms...

Every muscle in his body contracted in swift, violent desire. She only had to look at him to rouse that unsparing hunger.

But today she seemed...subdued, her glow dimmed, her face shadowed as though she'd lost some essential part of herself.

He said, 'I should have told you what I was planning to do. I'm sorry.'

Why had he not? He wasn't prepared to ask himself that question, nor to explore exactly why he felt uneasy. He had no difficulty in reading the moods of most people, but Rosemary was different; although she seemed bright and open on the surface, it was hard to know exactly what was going on behind that sunny face.

And that was all the apology she was likely to get, Rosie decided wryly as she accepted the glass and put it down on the table. Gerd had been born an autocrat, and his upbringing and position had simply grafted more formidable layers onto a nature already dominant and decisive.

He reached out a hand, palm uppermost. 'Am I forgiven?'

She put hers into it, watching as it was swallowed up in his tanned fingers. 'Marriage is—or should be—a partnership, even if by marrying you I automatically become your subject. And partners discuss things with each other.'

'I stand corrected.' He lifted her hand to his mouth and kissed it. Little rills of sensation ran up her arm, and her breath came shortly through her lips.

When he released her he said levelly, 'My private secretary will be arriving in a couple of hours. We'll be discussing how to organise the wedding, so of course you will sit in on the session.'

Rosie's heart dropped. His words made the future seem suddenly much closer. However, she'd been the one who wanted to know things. 'How long will it take for the wedding to be organised?'

'About a year,' he said casually. 'But first there will have to be an official betrothal ceremony. That will be a family occasion in the palace chapel, but it will mark the official start of our life together.'

An opinion that was echoed by the private secretary, a thin, middle-aged man who greeted her with a smile and a shrewd, although respectful survey. He'd probably expected someone six inches taller and elegant, she thought gloomily, someone whose family tree was clotted with titles.

The private secretary went on in his careful English, 'That will give us time to organise it in a suitable manner, and it will also give you, Ms Matthews, time to become known to the people of Carathia, to learn the language and become accustomed to us.' He smiled benignly at her. 'It will be a busy year for you, so it will travel fast.'

Clearly he thought she was panting to marry Gerd.

When the interview was over and the secretary had gone to another room to draft the final announcement, Gerd said, 'We need to make quite a few decisions before your mother arrives.'

'Like what?' she asked warily.

His smile lacked humour. 'Like a date.'

Faced so brutally with the impact of her agreement, she said, 'It won't really matter to me. I don't organise my diary a year ahead, and as far as I know Mother doesn't either.'

He nodded. 'Then there is the question of where you will live for this next year. I suggest that you move into Kelt's house in the capital. He has already agreed, but of course the decision must be yours. I will supply you with a household.'

Colour drained from her face. She closed her eyes for a moment and took a breath before opening them again. 'Gerd, this is not going to work. A *household*? I wouldn't know what to do with a household except the housework.'

'Calm down,' he advised. 'What has happened to that backbone of yours? I've always admired your courage and your resilience.'

Rosie flicked him a mutinous glance. 'Anyone can be courageous and resilient when it's not a matter of their entire future.'

But the compliment warmed her heart sufficiently for her to listen when he said calmly, 'I refuse to believe that the bold, gallant girl I know was just a sham. And this is not negotiable. This morning you made me a promise; I accepted your word and acted on it.'

If he said this once more she'd—she'd *bite* him! She must have been mad and she certainly wasn't going to tell him that this morning, still fogged with sex, she'd have promised him *anything*.

When she said nothing he went on, 'So it is decided. You'll need a social secretary who knows court etiquette. I have someone in mind for that, but the ultimate decision must be yours.'

'How hard is Carathian to learn?'

'It's difficult,' he admitted, 'but not impossible. You'll have lessons, and of course you'll hear it spoken all the time; you'll probably be surprised at how quickly you absorb it.'

'I can deal with learning the language,' she said trenchantly. 'But why did you feel obliged to force the issue? Do you need a wife—*any* wife—that much? And if you do, why on earth—when there must be a hundred or so women out there, much better equipped to deal with the sort of life you lead—did you pick on me?'

He sent her a look that should have quelled the tumbling words, but perhaps he recognised the hurt beneath them because his voice was almost gentle when he said, 'You know why.'

'Because we're good together in bed? How very shallow of you, Gerd!'

CHAPTER EIGHT

THE scorn in Rosie's voice should have flicked Gerd's imperturbable control, but his steady regard didn't waver. 'That is not the sole reason,' he stated, a cynical smile curling his mouth. 'I think you will make an excellent Grand Duchess once you've got used to the idea.'

He sank a hand into her curls, gently pulling her head back to expose the length of her throat, vulnerable and creamy. 'And we are more than *good* together,' he said in a low, abrasive voice that sent ripples of sensation through her, 'we are bloody sensational.'

Rosie closed her eyes against his intense, devouring gaze. 'Don't you dare use sex against me,' she said, but her tone lacked conviction, and she wasn't surprised by his rough purr of a laugh.

'Why not? It works so well,' he parried, and kissed the corner of her mouth, the lightest of kisses, so soft she barely felt it. 'And I give you licence to use it against me whenever you feel like it. I'd enjoy that.'

No doubt, because he wasn't a slave to his emotions. He didn't love her...

Her skin tightened at the drift of his particular scent, that faint, evanescent fragrance that somehow had the power to overwhelm her common sense. The ripples of excitement became torrents, converging, building, heating every cell into molten anticipation. Hunger was like a drug, a reckless need that stopped her brain from working and changed her into some infinitely wanton stranger.

She opened her eyes, miserably aware that the fire he summoned had burnt away the proud rejection she wanted to make. This was Gerd, and she loved him. More than that, she trusted him. He'd promised fidelity; she was sure he wouldn't break that vow.

And she couldn't think of anything she wanted more than to be his wife, to bear his children…

So she'd follow her heart. In time he might learn to love her as wholly, as completely as she loved him—arrogance and all, she thought wryly. But she'd have to learn to be content with what he could give her, and if that was his respect and his affection and his lovemaking—well, many women had settled for less and forged happy lives.

Neither of them had had a normal childhood; Gerd's parents had died young, and, although his grandmother had loved him, she'd been a distant figure, intent on matters of state. Rosie had grown up lacking the loving support most children took for granted. But she knew now that Gerd would be a good father, and together they'd make sure their children didn't lack the love and security that came when parents were in a committed, stable relationship.

He said quietly, 'I think it will be better if we don't make love until you are sure there will be no chance of pregnancy.'

'I—yes.' Her voice shook and she said fiercely, 'Why is everything so complicated?'

Without hesitation he answered, 'Life is complex, and made more so because we humans are a difficult lot, passionate and unreasonable and wanting things we know we shouldn't have.'

And Gerd was more complex than most.

Rosie glanced up to see him studying her face, his mouth disciplined into a straight, decisive line, eyes half-hidden by long lashes—yet not so impossible to read that she couldn't discern the speculation in them.

Did he suspect that she loved him?

The thought brought hot blood to her skin, so embarrassing that she turned her head away and walked across to the window to stare unseeingly out at the blue, blue sea.

What would she do if he could never match her feelings?

If she'd learned anything about him these past few days, it was that his duty to his country would always come first.

Looked at pragmatically, a wife who loved him would be perfect; that he didn't love her would give him the emotional freedom to concentrate on Carathia and its people and their welfare.

The thought of that was unbearably painful.

But hell, she thought cynically, the sex was good. No, it was more than good; as he'd said, it was fantastic. And she wasn't her mother, seeking an unattainable, fairy-tale love.

Or perhaps she was…

She turned her head and looked at him. He met her gaze, his eyes steady and direct.

Did she have the strength to walk away?

'I'll try not to disappoint you,' he said quietly.

Half a loaf is better than no bread.

The pragmatic, sensible thought popped into her brain from nowhere. How many times had she railed at it, demanding the whole loaf?

Now she realised she was going to accept what Gerd could offer.

Mind made up once and for all, she nodded. 'And I'll do my best not to disappoint you.'

Vows of eternal love weren't applicable, she thought ironically, yet this simple exchange went a little way to ease the hungry yearning inside her.

'So what happens now?' she asked.

'We go back to the capital.'

'Must we?' The words escaped before she had a chance to consider them.

'Much as I'd like to stay here, we have to.' Gerd's tone left no room for objections, but he softened slightly when he said, 'We need to have official portraits taken as soon as possible—tomorrow morning, in fact. My private secretary has organised a selection of clothes for you to choose from. I'd like you to wear something from a local designer.'

He paused as though expecting further objections, but Rosie nodded. That made sense. What didn't was the shiver of apprehension that chilled through her.

Gerd went on, 'In three days' time, once your mother and Alex and Hani and Kelt have arrived, there will be the official betrothal ceremony.' His expression indicated this was not negotiable. 'It's a traditional ceremony for family and friends, but you'll need to choose something to wear for that too—something formal.'

Startled, Rosie looked at his uncompromising face. 'As in long?'

'No. Formal day clothes—hat, gloves et cetera. I'm sure you know what sort of thing. If not, then the designer will advise you on the correct attire.'

Butterflies tumbled around in her stomach. 'It sounds as though this is a rehearsal for a wedding.'

'It's a long-standing tradition in the country, and a lot of people would feel the marriage was scarcely legal if it wasn't held.'

Reacting to his dismissive tone, Rosie asked tersely, 'Are there any other traditional occasions I need to know about?'

'Not immediately. After a week or so of festivities which we'll be expected to attend, things will settle down and you can move into Kelt's house.' He paused, then added, 'I suggest you ask your mother to stay with you for a month or so.'

'My *mother*?'

'She *is* your mother,' he reminded her coolly. 'Your only living relative apart from Alex.'

'Presumably this whole jolly family party thing is because it's important that my family—what there is of it—and yours are seen to accept the engagement?'

She couldn't bring herself to say 'our engagement'.

'That's part of it.' Gerd's voice didn't encourage her to go on, but she persisted.

'And the other part?'

He shrugged. 'After those damned photographs I want to put as official a slant on our holiday as it's possible to do.'

Rosie could see his point. In that photo they hadn't

looked like a betrothed couple. They'd looked as though they couldn't wait to get into bed together.

Although her nerves were strung tight and twanging, she gave a sparkling, mischievous grin. 'Oh,' she breathed, 'I can just see it now—this is going to be such fun! Mother can't resist provoking Alex in every way possible, but when he lifts that eyebrow of his and cuts her down to size with a few scathing words she loses her temper. And then—pouf! Fireworks to match that display we saw from your windows.'

'Don't worry. Alex will be fine.'

'It's not Alex I'm thinking of,' she told him prosaically.

Gerd's expression hardened. 'Your mother will be fine too,' he stated.

And she was. Oh, the tension was there—it always would be, Rosie suspected—but Eva was on her best behaviour, saving her comments for when she and Rosie were alone.

'I hope you know what you're doing,' she said, looking around the suite allotted to her.

Rosie said aloofly, 'Don't worry about that.'

Eva glanced at her. 'I know what it's like to marry the wrong man. I'd just as soon not watch you do it.'

Rosie felt uncomfortable. Her mother was a beauty, one of those rare women who defied the years, but her expression had settled into lines of petulance. She'd never spoken before of her husband and the marriage that had only lasted for a few years.

And Rosie didn't want to discuss it. Her father had been fond of her in his absent way; it seemed disloyal to listen to him being denigrated when he wasn't alive to defend himself.

'You won't be doing that,' she said with far more confidence than she felt.

Her mother shrugged. 'At least you're older—just—than I was when I married your father. But you have to realise that if you marry Gerd there'll be no divorce. The Carathians haven't progressed much since the Middle Ages. Their attitudes—especially in the mountain people—are still rock-solid conservative. If it doesn't work out you'll have to stick it out.'

When it doesn't work out, her tone implied. Before Rosie could say anything Eva went on, 'And, although there's huge prestige and glamour in being almost a queen, there must also be a lot of boredom.'

Struggling to control the tension that gripped her, Rosie said with a slight snap, 'I don't bore as easily as you do. And I didn't realise you knew so much about the Carathians.'

'Your father came here several times when he was married to Alex's mother.' Eva turned away to concentrate on the view out over the city and the mountains. 'He found them an interesting study. Until they discovered that stuff they mine for computers they were stuck in a kind of time warp—poverty-stricken and mediaeval. I can't see that thirty years of prosperity will have changed them that much.'

Possibly not, but Gerd's plans to educate them would help. Rosie said crisply, 'I'd already worked that out, although I doubt if they're quite as mediaeval as Father thought them.'

Her mother lifted her shoulders again. 'Very well, I've

said all I had to say. Now fill me in on what's going to happen.'

Briefly Rosie told her of the formal betrothal ceremony that would cement the engagement in the eyes of Gerd's subjects, and the events that would follow when she and Gerd would be on show.

'Quite a programme,' her mother said with a lift of her brows. 'Is Alex here?'

'He's landing in an hour or so.'

Her mother flashed her a taut smile. 'Don't look so concerned. I do know how to behave, even with Alex.'

Back in her own suite Rosie stood for a long moment with closed eyes, trying to control the turmoil of her emotions. What had she expected? That her mother would suddenly turn into someone able to offer advice and support?

It was never going to happen, and she'd accepted that long before she'd even understood what she needed from Eva.

She would, she thought with a quiver of apprehension, always be on her own.

But there would be children...

A tap on the door heralded Gerd, who after a moment's hard scrutiny demanded, 'What's the matter?'

'Nothing,' she said automatically, and to prove it flashed him a glance that was all challenge.

His brows rose, but he said blandly, 'Can you come along to my office and look over some rings I've had sent up?'

At her startled glance he added with a smile, 'Even in the wilderness of Carathia we have engagement rings.'

'Oh,' she said, and managed to produce a laugh that sounded unconvincing. 'I hadn't thought of rings.'

His gaze was uncomfortably keen. 'Then think of it now.'

'And Carathia isn't a wilderness,' she said briskly, still resenting her mother's comments.

Gerd held out his hand. 'Come here,' he said, his eyelashes drooping in a way that made her heart thud erratically.

Flushing, she went into his arms. He seemed to understand she needed comfort more than the erotic flashfire of passion, because he just held her, his cheek on the top of her head. Sighing, Rosie relaxed against him, taking immense comfort from his solid male strength and the warmth of his arms around her.

Eventually he said, 'Better?'

Feeling a little foolish, she murmured, 'Yes, I'm fine.'

He let her go, but retained her hand as they left the room.

In his office a tray of rings glittered against the black velvet of their case. Stunned, Rosie drew in a deep breath.

Gerd said, 'Although diamonds are the convention, I thought golden ones would suit you better than ones with blue fire. But if you don't like them the stones can be replaced.'

'I love them,' she said quietly, and then laughed as she scanned them. 'All of them! What an impossible choice!'

'Well, we can sort them out. A stone too big will weigh that elegant finger down, so these can go.'

He indicated three large solitaires.

Colour burned along Rosie's cheekbones. The last time he'd referred to her hands it had been about their effect on him when they made love.

'You agree?' Gerd asked.

'Yes.' How she wished she were tall and graceful and gorgeous, like the two women she knew had been Gerd's lovers. Neither of them had uncontrollable red curls; both had worn smooth dark hair pulled back from superb features, and they'd breathed a sophisticated intelligence.

Clearly he was accustomed to choosing jewellery. So what had he chosen for those women—rings? Probably not, she thought acidly. Rings might be taken to mean commitment. Necklaces? Or bracelets?

Whatever, anything he'd given his lovers had been chosen because he'd wanted them, and not for reasons of state. Hot jealousy—and a bitter spurt of envy—tightened her nerves.

'Something special,' Gerd said. He indicated one in particular. 'Do you like this?'

How had he known that of them all, this was the one she'd have chosen for herself? The stone wasn't huge, but it shone like the heart of summer, an intense honeyed glow that made the others pale.

'It's beautiful,' Rosie said. But a ring as exquisite as that should be a token of love.

He plucked it from the velvet and held it out. 'Try it on,' he invited.

Rosie hesitated, then held out her hand and watched numbly as he slid it onto her ring finger.

Gerd thought that it looked as though it had been made for her, the colour of the stone echoing the sunlit vibrancy of her skin and curls, the glints of gold that usually danced in her eyes.

He watched her face as the ring slid home, saw her mouth tighten and then relax, and wondered again just what was going on in her brain.

She was, he thought grimly, driving him mad. Previously he'd enjoyed civilised affairs; he'd liked his lovers and made sure they understood the limits he set on relationships. They'd been passionate enough to keep him interested, but not so intense that hunger took over his mind and got between him and his work.

Rosemary was different. From the start she'd defied all his rules, starting with that long holiday three years previously when he'd really got to know her. Slowly, insidiously his affection for the girl-child he'd known all her life had metamorphosed into a forbidden desire, one he was determined not to act on.

He'd restrained himself until the night before he'd left for Carathia, but something snapped then, and he'd taken an irrevocable step. It had been meant to be one kiss, and a very light one, but her sensuous response had knocked him sideways. The dangerous surge of desire it summoned had eaten away at his self-control; it had taken every particle of willpower he possessed to lift his head and lower his arms and step away from her, and afterwards he'd spent a sleepless night trying to deal with his reaction.

When he'd seen her kissing Kelt just as ardently it had been like a savage betrayal, one he'd vowed never to forget.

Discovering that she'd stayed a virgin had surprised him. More dangerously, the knowledge had satisfied something unregenerate and primal in him, stripping away his defences so that all he could think of was his craving for her.

In his arms she was wildfire and wine and erotic fulfilment, and he couldn't get enough of her.

Rosie looked up and caught the hunger in Gerd's gaze, a lick of fire that flared at her instant response. The hairs lifted on the back of her neck while adrenalin surged through her, and her eyes darkened.

He smiled, a tight, fierce movement of his lips, and said softly, 'Perfect.'

And raised her hand and kissed the ring, and then her palm. Exciting little shivers scudded the length of her spine.

More than anything Rosie wanted him to kiss her properly, but he resisted the vibration that sizzled between them and released her hand. Her pleasure evaporating, she looked down at the ring weighing her finger down like a badge of office.

Exactly what it was, she thought.

He said, 'So that's the betrothal ring. What sort of wedding band do you think would go with that?'

'I—don't know.' She looked down at the small sun glittering on her finger. 'I've barely had time to appreciate this gorgeous thing, and now you want me to choose a wedding ring?'

'It's traditional.'

'I thought that in Europe they didn't have the same traditions we do.'

'There has always been a wedding ring, and when my grandfather gave my grandmother an engagement ring, the first one in Carathia, every woman in the country wanted one as well,' he said drily.

Rosie thought a moment, her eyes fixed on the golden diamond. 'How about a ring with an inlaid silver pattern?' she suggested.

'Perhaps you could discuss it with the designer. He is waiting for us. You will need other jewels, of course.' His voice altered fractionally. 'Will you object to wearing some of the royal collection?'

'No.' Her voice whispered into the room. Burdened as she was by the reality of marrying Gerd, the royal collection of jewels somehow seemed a symbol of all that would be different in her life from now on.

Well, she'd agreed. So she swallowed and said more audibly, 'No, of course I won't.'

'There is an abundance to choose from,' he told her negligently. 'I'll make a selection of pieces you might like, and you can decide which ones you really like. Some are distinctly old-fashioned, so possibly they'll need resetting.'

The designer, a solid middle-aged man, bowed when he was introduced and wished them every happiness. He approved her choice of ring, and when asked about a wedding band whipped out a pencil and a pad and sketched something for her.

'I'm not sure about the roses,' she said, examining it. 'My name is Rosemary, not Rose.'

The designer looked chagrined. 'I'm sorry—'

Gerd intervened. 'Myrtle.' He smiled down at Rosie, his acting so good she could almost believe for a moment that he loved her. 'You liked it, didn't you, and because it and New Zealand's pohutukawa are very distant cousins, it will provide a link with your homeland?'

Of course, roses stood for love, whereas myrtle was sacred to Aphrodite, the goddess of passion and desire...

Rosie's answering smile was restrained. 'Oh, yes, how suitable.'

Gerd gave her a sharp glance, but the designer nodded. 'A charming idea.' Rapidly he sketched another design, then regarded it with a smile before handing it over to Gerd. 'Yes—the simpler the design the more effective.'

After he'd left Rosie said, 'That was an inspired suggestion.'

'You appeared to enjoy the scent of the sprigs of myrtle you picked,' Gerd said dismissively. Then he smiled down at her. 'Besides, we made some very pleasant memories there the day you first saw it.'

Her heart expanding, Rosie smiled back. 'So we did,' she said.

Surely, he couldn't look at her like that if he didn't feel something for her!

Buoyed by that idea, she almost enjoyed posing for the set of official photographs, even though it took almost half a day before the photographer was satisfied.

'I don't do dignity well,' Rosie sighed to Gerd when it was over. She glanced down at her clothes—a dress from a local designer that managed to be both formal and summery. 'But I love this and the other clothes that have come. Only...who is paying for them?'

'I am,' he told her calmly. 'And I think you do dignity very well. Dignity—but with warmth and interest.'

Right then she couldn't appreciate the compliment. 'I don't think you should be paying for my clothes,' she objected.

He looked at her, his expression uncompromising. 'I've already had this conversation with your brother,' he said inflexibly. 'I don't intend to go through it again with you.'

'I don't want either of you—'

'Rosemary, just leave it, will you?' His eyes were as crystalline and cold as the diamond she wore. 'You are in this position because I asked you to be, and so it is up to me to see that you have everything you need.'

'Gerd, we are not going to get along at all well if you tell me to leave things instead of discussing them sensibly,' she said through her teeth. 'If I'm old enough to marry you, damn it, I'm old enough to be consulted about things that might seem trifles to you but are important to me. It's disrespectful and unfair and patronising if we can only discuss things that are important to you!'

He looked down at her as though he'd been bitten by a kitten, then unexpectedly gave a wry smile. 'You are, of course, correct. Very well, then, explain to me how it will make you feel better if neither Alex nor I pay for the clothes you need for formal occasions.'

He had a point. But so did she. Rosie drew in a breath and said, 'I'm not in the same league financially as you or Alex, but I do have a little money in the bank. I can at least use that.'

'I would like you to keep it so that you don't feel entirely dependent on me.'

Neither yielding, they measured glances. Rosie was

torn by indecision. In the end she said, 'I realise it seems quixotic, but—'

'It's a statement of independence?'

Actually, it probably was—a symbolic answer to the ring on her finger and all it represented. 'It's more that you just made the assumption that you'd pay without even talking it over with me.'

He nodded. 'I won't make that mistake again. But there is something we need to discuss right now. You will need an allowance.'

Rosie opened her mouth but before she could speak he said lazily, 'I shall feel compelled to kiss any further objections away, and you know where that will lead.'

Heat coloured her skin, but her eyes stayed steady. 'That is sexist. And two can play at that game.'

His eyes narrowed. 'Feel free, any time,' he invited silkily.

CHAPTER NINE

Rosie glared at him, then closed her eyes in surrender. 'You don't play fair.'

'Neither do you.' Gerd's voice was low and amused and very, very sexy.

Her eyes opened and she warded him off with up-raised hands. 'As it happens, I wasn't going to object to an allowance,' she said forthrightly. 'But I'll use my own money until it's gone.'

Gerd shrugged. 'You're not going to budge on this, are you?'

'No.'

'And you don't want me to try and persuade you…?' He let the suggestion hang in the air.

'I do not,' she told him as crisply as she could.

Which was not very effective. Her voice had softened, and the lazy, languorous note in it constituted a far from subtle invitation.

He knew, of course, that if he touched her, kissed her, she'd melt, and then she'd be lost. But he had to accept that he couldn't just make decisions for her and expect her to obey them without question.

So she repeated coolly, 'I can see the point of an allowance, so I'll accept that. But until my money runs out I'll buy my own clothes.'

'Your personal clothes,' he conceded. 'Anything you need to buy for official occasions will come from your household expenses.'

'Very well,' she said reluctantly.

He frowned. 'Are you always going to be like this?'

'I suspect I am.' A little acidly she went on, 'Feel like changing your mind?'

His face hardened. 'No.'

The evening before the betrothal ceremony he gave a dinner at the palace, where he introduced Rosie to his personal friends. It was a relaxed occasion, without formal speeches or toasts, but Rosie realised she was being assessed.

Afterwards Gerd dropped a light kiss on her forehead at her bedroom door. 'Sleep well,' he said.

'I'm scared,' she blurted, regretting the words as soon as they escaped. 'What if nobody likes me?'

He gave her a hug, but immediately freed her and stepped back. 'Has anyone ever disliked you?' he asked rhetorically.

Her mother, for one. 'Jo Green in Year Three hated me,' Rosie told him. 'She used to pinch me and call me Ginge.'

He laughed. 'Nobody will do that here.'

More seriously she said, 'I suppose what's really concerning me is that I simply might not be able to do the job with the sort of—well, gravitas that it needs. I don't want to fail you or your people.'

'I didn't realise that beneath that self-assured manner you're lacking in confidence.'

She shrugged. 'It is an unusual situation, and one I haven't been trained for.' Unlike Princess Serina, who probably wouldn't dream of dumping her insecurities on her chosen spouse, no matter who he was.

Gerd said calmly, 'I have complete faith in your ability to deal with anything.'

Rosie looked up, her heart thumping erratically. *So why don't you kiss me?* But he wasn't going to use that simplest of ways to comfort her. He seemed to have pulled up some emotional drawbridge, leaving her alone and forlorn on the other side.

Gerd said, 'Tomorrow morning after the ceremony a crowd might gather in front of the palace.'

'Why?' she asked blankly.

'To wish us joy. We will come out as a family and wave from the balcony off the grand drawing room.' He smiled at her startled look. 'So perhaps you will need even higher heels than usual so they can see you over the balustrade.'

'I'm not that short,' she said indignantly.

'Just as high as my heart,' he quoted.

Rosie smiled and closed the door on him, but her smile faded quickly into wistfulness. She wished—oh, how she wished—he wouldn't say things like that.

Not when he didn't really mean them…

Her dress for the official betrothal was already hanging in her dressing room, a silk in a champagne colour that just skimmed her body and made her feel elegant and tall. And fortunately her sandals had very high heels. The hat was cut so that everyone could see her face.

A knock on the door brought heat to her cheeks and

an aching hunger to her heart—a feverish anticipation that was dashed when her mother came in.

'Is anything wrong?' she asked.

'No.' Her mother noted the dress hanging ready to be worn, and said, 'Very appropriate. You get your taste from me. Your father didn't care about clothes.'

Rosie told her what Gerd had said about a crowd collecting, and her mother nodded. 'Oh, yes, I've been forewarned about it.'

'I doubt if it's going to happen. Why would they?'

'Curiosity,' her mother said dismissively. She paused, then said deliberately, 'I wouldn't take it personally. You could have two heads and they'd be delighted. What they want is children from you— preferably boys.'

Rosie lifted her brows. 'I suppose they do,' she said quietly, determined not to let her mother see how much that hurt. 'The succession has to be important.'

'It's hugely important in any monarchy, but for Gerd it's vital.'

'I know.' And because she didn't want to go into the reasons Gerd needed heirs, she said, 'Mother, Gerd and I discussed the situation before I agreed to marry him. And even if we hadn't, as you said a couple of days ago, it's too late to back out now.'

Eva said in dismay, 'Don't tell me he's convinced you that he's in love with you!'

At Rosie's steady gaze her mother looked slightly shamefaced, but she kept on with a bitter twist to her lips. 'And even knowing that he's going to use you as a baby machine, you still decided to marry him? Are you pregnant?'

Rosie kept her head high. 'No.'

'And there I always thought you were a runaway romantic,' her mother said with heavy irony.

Rosie's smile was twisted. 'No, you're the runaway romantic.'

'Forget about me. Don't try to persuade me that you're marrying him for the prestige and the money. I know you've been infatuated with him since you were eighteen.'

Please go right now. But Rosie couldn't say the words.

Her mother looked at her with an expression she'd never seen before.

'I've made a mess of my life,' she said abruptly. 'I married your father too young—I thought he loved me, but all he wanted was to go off on his various expeditions without having to bother about organising child care for Alex. He never got over losing his first wife. Oh, he was quite pleased when I had you, although he'd have preferred another boy, but we weren't important to him—his research was. Even Alex came a pretty poor second to that.'

'I'm sorry,' Rosie said quietly. 'But it's not like that with Gerd and me.'

'Gerd is…well, everything a woman could want, but he's going to be married to Carathia.'

'I know.'

'I hope you do,' her mother said bleakly. 'Otherwise you'll eat your heart out wanting something that's never going to happen.'

But that was exactly what she was going to do, Rosie realised in the sleepless hours that followed her mother's awkward departure. Thoughts raced through her head, jumbled and anguished, filled with emotions so painful she couldn't bear them.

Eventually she got up and walked across to the window. It would be simpler—and easier—if she didn't love Gerd.

She looked down on the darkened, silent city, the street lamps lonely beacons, starshine glimmering on a jumble of tiled roofs and the slick of wet concrete.

Why had her mother's words unsettled her so much? Easy—they'd struck home only because Rosie was more accustomed to exasperation than concern from her mother.

And away from Gerd's compelling presence, without the gloss of sexual passion clouding her brain, Gerd's proposal and her response seemed a cold, bleakly practical reaction to the situation they'd found themselves in.

Her hand drifted across to touch her waist. What if she couldn't have children?

Too late to worry about that now...

The words echoed in her head as she got back into bed and drifted off to a restless sleep.

Church bells woke her—a joyous cacophony that soared up from the city's churches. She sat straight up in bed, head aching slightly, then got up and inched the heavy curtains open a fraction. Although it was barely past dawn—in fact, over the mountains she saw the last star wink out—already people were moving in the streets below.

Heading towards the palace.

'Oh, lord,' she muttered, yanking the drapes closed in case anyone saw her peeking.

A knock on her door whirled her around. The maid who looked after her clothes came in, beaming when Rosie greeted her. With a little bob she said carefully, 'A beautiful day for us all in Carathia. I wish you great happiness, my lady.'

Rosie's nerves tightened painfully, her sense of doom increasing as the morning wound on. Although a betrothal ceremony was usually restricted to family and closest friends, because of Gerd's position there would be politicians and important people there too. All dressed to the nines, she realised when she was escorted into the front pew with Eva, who was slim and soignée in one of the vibrant colours she wore so well.

At least Kelt and Hani and their little Rafi sat with them, with Alex, saturnine as usual. And the service was short; it involved a blessing, the ceremonial bestowal of the ring by Gerd, dark and unsmiling as he slid it onto her finger, and the exchange of a kiss before the altar—both the kiss and Gerd's attitude being studiously impersonal. A brief homily from the priest, delivered in Carathian, was clearly an exposition of what was expected of them. Unable to understand, aware of Gerd's withdrawal beside her, Rosie had never felt so alone.

But walking back down the aisle with him beside her, part of a procession featuring candles and crosses, and choirboys who sang like angels, it warmed her to meet the smiles of those who'd been at last night's dinner.

And at the reception that followed, Gerd's approving nod and murmured words of appreciation, his hand in the small of her back, restored her confidence. It helped that most of the people used their store of English to converse with her. As a child Gerd and Kelt had taught her the conventional greetings and farewells in Carathian, but beyond those she understood nothing of the language as yet.

Language lessons, and soon, she decided sturdily.

Eventually the family was marshalled into order in the drawing room. Stomach flipping, she shivered at the murmur of the crowd in the huge square below.

'It sounds as though everyone in the city is out there,' she said to Gerd.

'Just about,' he said. 'Come on, it's time to go.' He looked down and his serious expression lightened. 'How do you manage to walk in those heels?'

'It's a technique small girls study from the first time they try on their mother's shoes,' she said, repressing another, quite different shiver at the glint in his gaze. 'By the time they reach adolescence it's completely automatic.'

And then it was time to move out onto the balcony. The hairs on the back of her neck lifted at the sight of the people packed into the square and the wild roar that greeted them as they moved across to the balustrade. Everyone in that huge, seething mass of people seemed to be waving something—brightly coloured streamers, flowers and handkerchiefs.

And the noise was indescribable—breathtaking and almost terrifying, except that everyone seemed to be smiling.

Gerd looked down at her. 'Smile, Rosemary. This is for you.'

But it wasn't. His people loved and respected him;

they trusted him to marry a person who would fit into their world, and they believed she was that person.

Then and there, Rosie decided that such trust deserved to be honoured. She would become the person the Carathians believed her to be.

'Nonsense—they don't know me at all. This is all for you,' she said, and pinned a smile to her lips as she waved back.

Gerd said coolly, 'The Chief Minister has suggested that we travel into the mountains next week. The people there have a tendency to feel neglected.'

And that, of course, was where the last rebellion had been fomented. Rosie's stomach clenched, but she nodded and smiled brightly up at him, only dimly hearing the renewed burst of cheering that provoked.

Gerd said, 'We'll visit the largest town there, and it would be politic to go down to the coast.'

'That sounds great,' she said, waving again at the excited, happy mass of people who seemed determined to let their ruler know they shared his happiness.

His *supposed* happiness, Rosie corrected herself.

The crowd cheered anew and began throwing their flowers and ribbons in a shower of colour into the sparkling, sunlit air until eventually Gerd said, 'Time to go.'

With a final wave the family turned and filed back inside, adjourning to Gerd's private apartments, where they were served lunch.

Kelt gave Rosie a hug, saying, 'Thank you.'

'For what?'

He grinned. 'For taking Gerd on. I didn't realise it, but he needs someone like you—he's far too autocratic, and you'll keep him on his toes. And the Carathians will love you.'

Rosie laughed, but his words made her feel oddly disconnected, as though by marrying Gerd she'd turn into a different person.

She glanced across the room and saw Gerd watching them, his face impassive. Something tight and hard contracted inside her. He looked bleak and almost angry.

But only for a second. When he caught her eye he lifted his brows and came towards them and, as always, her breath shortened and she felt that secret heat stirring in her body.

Kelt gave him a brotherly cuff on the shoulder. 'About time,' he said obscurely.

Gerd's brows climbed again. 'I think Hani wants you,' he said.

Both Rosie and Gerd watched Kelt set off purposefully across the huge, gilt-decorated drawing room to his wife, who was perched on the edge of an ornate sofa. Hani's face lit up when her husband approached.

Pierced by a depressing envy and a feeling of intruding on something special between Kelt and his wife, Rosie turned away. 'It looked as though most of the city was there this morning.'

Gerd's voice was coolly non-committal. 'Quite a few,' he agreed. 'How do you feel?'

'Fine,' she said, surprising herself with the realisation. 'The betrothal ceremony made me realise that I need to start learning the language straight away, but you don't need words to wave from a balcony!' She thought for a moment, then said, 'I feel welcomed. Which sounds silly, because that crowd gathered for you, not me, but everyone there looked warm-hearted and pleased for us both.'

'Carathians enjoy a good party.' Although he smiled down at her, his eyes were still remote. 'And you were welcomed, and are welcome. You did very well.'

His words should have warmed her, but the more legalities bound them together, she thought unhappily, the more distant Gerd became. She wondered if they would ever regain the laughter and burgeoning closeness, the thrilling hope, of those few crazy, passion-filled days on the island.

So far away they seemed now, so impossible to retrieve...

The next day Kelt and Hani took her to the town house, and for a little while she could relax in their undemanding company, playing with their little boy before being shown over the old, beautifully appointed building.

'I hope you enjoy living here,' Hani said, looking around. 'Kelt said it was still firmly Victorian until he inherited it; he had all the plumbing and wiring redone, and when we got married I organised the most hideous of the furniture into storage. We don't stay here much because of that legend, but it's very comfortable. And the Carathians are very kind.'

'Hani, it's lovely. Both you and Kelt have done a great job on it. But even nicer is that I can feel your presence here.'

Hani smiled mistily at her. 'Dear Rosie,' she said. 'We're all going to miss you like crazy, but I think the Carathians already know how lucky they are to have you.'

To Rosie's horror she felt tears sting her eyes. 'Thank

you,' she said on a gulp. 'Oh, hell, I never cry—this is ridiculous. I'll miss you too, even though I expect to see lots of you and Kelt and little Rafi.'

She waved them off the next morning, with her mother, as they were all travelling back to New Zealand together. 'I have to tidy things up at home,' Eva said briskly, 'and then I'll be back.'

Rosie said, 'I know it will be a sacrifice for you. Thank you.'

Eva looked a little startled. With a hint of sarcasm she said, 'I didn't make any sacrifices for you as a child, so it's probably only fair that I should now.'

They looked at each other for a moment. Eva shrugged and went on, 'We should be able to live together for a couple of months without coming to blows.'

'I can't see why not. We're both adults,' Rosie said firmly.

'Think of it as training for all the sacrifices you're going to make for Carathia,' her mother advised.

In spite of that, Eva's attitude gave Rosie hope that perhaps she and her mother could form some sort of relationship.

'Not a real mother-daughter relationship,' she said to Gerd as they travelled back from the airport. 'But some sort of friendly association. She's changed.'

'How?' he asked, his tone disbelieving.

'She's a little softer—just as cynical, but somehow not so bitter. And there's no man in tow, yet she doesn't seem to care.'

Gerd leaned back in the car. 'Let's hope it lasts. Are you ready for our quick tour of the mountains?'

'Yes. Will the white lily be blooming?' She wanted very much to see Carathia's national flower.

'It's usually over by now, but there might be some pockets of it left.'

There were, and after an excited and friendly reception from the people who'd flocked into the biggest town in the mountain region, they flew by helicopter up to the edge of the winter snowline.

'There, my lady,' the guide said, indicating a plant nestled in against a rock.

Rosie gave an excited squeak and crouched down. Fragile and fleeting, white petals airily danced above the grim rocks and the matted tangle of its leaves.

'They're tough, aren't they?' Rosie said, crouching beside it. Carefully she stroked the flower, wondering at the resilience of such a lovely thing in this hard landscape.

The botanist and the mountaineer who'd accompanied them both nodded, the botanist saying in her limited English, 'Strong and beautiful—like the mountains.'

'Like Carathians,' the mountain guide said proudly. He glanced at Gerd, and said something in their language.

Gerd translated as Rosie stood up. 'He's recited a local proverb that compares a beautiful woman to the summer sun, warming the eyes and the heart.' His smile was swift. 'He means you.'

Rosie flushed. 'Thank you very much,' she said to the guide, who made a little bow.

She and Gerd could afford only a short time there in the cool, crisp air, and too soon they were back in the helicopter. As they swooped down into the valley, Rosie hugged the memory of the flowers and the look in Gerd's eyes when he relayed the guide's compliment.

Whatever his reason for keeping such a distance between them, it was not because he didn't want her. For a precious second she had seen a flare of passionate need turn his eyes to gold.

That night they attended a formal dinner with the local dignitaries before returning to the hotel, a large, tourist-oriented building, where they occupied the whole top floor. Dismissing her maid, Rosie got ready for bed, only to be surprised by a knock on the door.

Gerd?

And it *was* him. Her heart pumping into overdrive, she opened the door wider. 'Come in,' she said, hoping, hoping...and then hoping her eyes didn't betray her disappointment when he shook his head.

'Kelt's on the telephone,' he said. 'He's being put through to your phone, but I thought I'd warn you.'

'Warn me?' Instantly her confusion and hope were banished by fear. 'Is anything wrong?'

'No, but he has news for you.'

Bewildered, Rosie closed the door behind him and went back to the telephone, anxiously waiting for it to ring. When the sound burred into the quiet air she snatched up the receiver and said urgently, 'Kelt?'

'Rosie. I just thought I'd ring to tell you that Hani and I are expecting another baby.'

So relieved her knees felt weak, she collapsed onto the sofa. 'Oh, Kelt, that's wonderful! I did wonder while she was here—a couple of times she looked a bit peaky, but I thought maybe she was just tired. So when's the baby due?'

'In six months' time,' he said cheerfully.

'And you're still determined not to know what sex it is?'

'Absolutely. Hani says the desire to find out is the only thing that keeps her going through labour and the birth.'

The tenderness beneath the laughter in his voice made Rosie blink back tears, but she retorted, 'I don't believe that for a moment. Kelt, that's fantastic news! I'm so glad for you and for Hani. Can I say hello to her?'

'Actually she's in bed—no, she's all right, it's just that this one does seem to make her more tired than Rafi did. She's fine, and once you're back in the capital she'll ring and you can have a nice, long, feminine gossip.'

Rosie was laughing as she put the telephone back into the cradle, but her laughter faded, and unbidden, painful tears scalded her eyes and clogged her throat.

A familiar loneliness seeped through her, draining her of strength. She fought it with everything she could, but the tears came just the same, slowly falling. It was horrible to cry because Hani was going to have a baby.

She said aloud, 'No, it's not the baby.'

Her stupid tears were because Hani's children were the product of a union completely different from the marriage she had agreed to. When she was with Kelt and Hani it was impossible not to feel that unworthy envy of their profound and enduring love for each other. Their children were not symbols, not conceived to hold together a country.

For the first time Rosie wondered about the children she and Gerd would have—would they hate living in the royal fishbowl, wish they'd been ordinary children born to ordinary parents and an ordinary life, able to work out their own destiny instead of being chained by tradition and the needs and expectations of millions of people?

The door opened and she turned, gulping back her tears, but it was too late. Gerd stood there, looking at her, his expression unreadable.

He walked into the room, closed the door behind him, and asked curtly, 'I knocked, but you didn't hear me. What's happened?'

'Nothing. I m-must be tired, I think,' she said, and wiped her eyes with one hand, looking around vainly for tissues.

Gerd came across and dropped an unused handkerchief into her lap. 'Use this,' he commanded, and walked over to the window.

She eyed his silhouette, big and lithe and forbiddingly distant, and her heart ached painfully in her breast. She loved him so much, yet it wasn't enough. If only she knew what it was that had made him decide to pull further and further away from her.

Without looking at her he said, 'Kelt told you his news?'

'Yes. It's lovely for them both, isn't it.'

'Is that why you were crying?'

Rosie flinched, then looked up anxiously. He'd turned and was watching her, but she could gain nothing from his expression. 'No,' she said too quickly. 'No, of course it's not. I'm thrilled for them. Hani's always said she wanted four children.'

She very much wanted to get to her feet, to draw herself up to her full height, but she didn't trust her legs to sustain her.

Anyway, she thought wearily, who was she kidding? Her full height was far from impressive.

Gerd said, 'I thought you'd got over Kelt.'

CHAPTER TEN

AT FIRST Gerd's words didn't register. Oh, Rosie heard them, but their meaning escaped her. 'What?'

He shrugged. 'It was always obvious you had a terrific crush on him.'

Rosie went white. It was so ludicrous an idea, so distant from what he must—surely—know already?

He went on, 'I admired the fact that you took his marriage to Hani so well. Was it because you knew you had to if you were going to be able to stay as close to him?'

Stunned, she said, 'No!'

His brows lifted. Dispassionately he went on, 'Because you must know by now that it's no use. He and Hani are not just husband and wife, they're lovers and soul-mates.'

'I know that.' Afraid that she sounded defensive rather than convincing, she hurried on, 'But you're utterly wrong—couldn't be *more* wrong. I've never been in love with Kelt.'

He said tersely, 'Don't lie to me, Rosemary. I can cope with almost anything but lies, and we made a promise to be honest with each other, remember?'

A kind of wild hope mingled with enough anger to revive Rosie. Scrambling up, she said in a rough voice,

'I am being totally and completely honest with you! Of course I love Kelt—he's the big brother I didn't have, almost the *father* I didn't have! He's always been there for me. But *in love* with him? Where on earth did you get that idea?'

'I always knew you had a crush on him, but what clinched the fact was that the morning after we kissed—you and I—I came out onto the terrace at the homestead and saw you and Kelt walking up from the horse paddock.' His voice was chilling and detached. 'You hurled yourself into his arms and kissed him passionately.'

The colour drained from her skin, then flooded back. 'Oh, hell,' she said, and then started to laugh. It came too close to turning into a sob, but she managed to choke it back and meet his eyes defiantly. 'I was conducting a scientific experiment.'

He said blankly, 'What?'

'You heard.' She dragged in a breath and explained, 'You'd kissed me the night before, and—well, I was eighteen, but I'd never experienced anything like it before.' She spread her hands helplessly. 'Bells rang and sky-rockets soared and stars exploded, and I was—I was *transported*. But I didn't know anything about grown-up kisses, and after worrying about it all night I decided to kiss Kelt and see if it happened all over again.'

Gerd's face was a mixture of emotions, none of which she could read. When he spoke his voice was hard and demanding. 'And what did happen?'

'Nothing,' she said simply. 'Nothing at all. It was creepy, actually. And he was shocked until I told him what I was doing it for, and then he laughed, but he told me not to let myself get too interested in you because I was far too young for you.'

'And he warned me off,' Gerd said harshly. 'We were talking at cross purposes, of course, and I thought he was interested in you.'

'He met Hani just after that, so you must have realised then he wasn't,' she pointed out, a cautious hope warming her heart.

'And you weren't in love with him?'

'No,' she said explosively. 'Of course I wasn't—never have been! OK, I can understand how that incident the night after we kissed must have looked—I'll bet you thought I was a little tramp—but you must have known that for me Kelt has only ever been my substitute brother.'

'It just seemed…logical. As you say, he looked out for you. It would have been unusual if you didn't see him as your particular hero. And you've always been openly affectionate with him.'

'Well, yes, but it never meant anything! Surely—'

'When he and Hani left after the coronation you were upset.'

'Of course, I was sad to see them go.' She was talking too fast, the words tumbling over each other. Afraid to allow herself to hope, she willed him to believe her. 'I've been almost part of their family—a sort of feckless younger sister, really.'

She scanned his handsome face for any sign of softening.

Not a thing. Still in that cool, judicial voice, he said, 'So why were you crying? I know Kelt rang you especially to tell you Hani is pregnant.'

Torn, Rosie almost put her emotions into words, but instinct warned her that it would be too dangerous to reveal her love for him, her abject reliance on him...

Lamely she said, 'There are happy tears as well as sad ones.'

'You can go,' he said abruptly.

Her heart turned to lead. She stared disbelievingly at him, overwhelmed with such anguish she could barely form the words. 'What...where?'

'Go home.' His words were delivered precisely, as icy as the metallic gold in his eyes.

'But I can't.' The foolish words barely registered in her mind. Pain sliced through her, numbing her brain, freezing her soul.

'You can. I'll organise a flight for you out of the country tomorrow.' And when she didn't move he said stonily, 'It's not going to work, so it's better to cut our losses now—before it's too late.'

Unable to respond, she stared at his ruthless, inflexible face.

He lifted one clenched fist and slammed it down on the windowsill. 'Go,' he said between his teeth. 'Go now, before—'

The flicker of hope encouraged her enough to say unevenly, 'Before what?'

'It doesn't matter. I'll ring your maid—'

She fanned that tiny glimmer of courage. This was too important for her not to fight for what she wanted. 'I need to know,' she said. 'Before what?'

'Before we end up hating each other.'

He wasn't looking at her, but his stance, his coiled strength, revealed a man with every muscle on the alert.

'Gerd,' she said, risking everything, 'tell me one thing—and remember our promise of honesty to each other. What do you feel for me?'

White-lipped, he stared at her. Rosie's breath stopped in her throat but she didn't dare back down. This was too important.

'You really want your pound of flesh, don't you?' he ground out eventually. 'Very well, then, you deserve to know. I love you.'

Rosie's incandescent blaze of joy was dowsed when he went on grimly, 'I love you desperately enough to have abandoned all my principles and more or less forced you into an engagement you didn't want, and a life I knew you hated the thought of. I told myself you couldn't respond so passionately to me if you didn't feel something more than lust. I knew it was less than love, but I was prepared to accept what I could get from you.'

How blind he was! Unsteadily she asked, 'So if you love me, why are you sending me away?'

CHAPTER ELEVEN

GERD's head came up. In his most arrogant tone he said, 'I love you too much—I can't bear to see you unhappy. Your tears rip my heart out.'

Sheer ecstasy burst through Rosie like a nova, the glory of his words wiping out everything else. Unable to speak, she stared at him with dilating eyes.

Even more harshly he went on, 'I find in myself a certain distaste for pleading. But I have an even greater distaste of forcing you into a situation that causes you such misery.' He paused, then went on in the same level tone, 'Therefore I release you from your promise, and I wish you every happiness in the future.'

Gazing at his face—still pale beneath the tan, its framework boldly angular and forceful—she realised she'd managed to hide her feelings so well he had no idea of them. Somehow she had to convince him that his love, given with such reluctance, was matched and returned by her.

'Gerd, you *idiot*!' she said when she could control her voice. 'I was crying because Hani is pregnant, and I wasn't.'

He looked at her as though she were mad. 'What has that to do with anything?'

'I envy them like crazy, and I was wishing it was the same for us—that no-holds-barred kind of love and trust and respect.' Freed from anguish now, she said, 'I love you! How could you not know that? And if you send me away, I'll probably end up like my mother.'

'What the hell do you mean by that?' he demanded. 'You're nothing like your mother.'

She took a deep breath. 'Maybe not, but she did love my father in the beginning.'

'So she says,' he said caustically, and then, 'And what on earth has she to do with us?'

'I believe her,' Rosie told him. 'He couldn't return her love, so she left him. If you send me away I won't set off on a useless search for a love to replace the one I can't have. But I'll never marry anyone else, never love anyone as I love you. So if you don't want me to be your wife and have your children—'

'Don't *want* you?' he demanded in a voice she'd never heard before. 'I want you so much it's eating my heart out.' He made a quick, unconsidered gesture and said something low and angry before striding across the room towards her.

Not knowing what to expect, Rosie quivered, but she held her head high and met his eyes without flinching. Everything, she thought, hinged on these moments. Her whole life…

He stopped a pace away. In a raw, undisciplined voice he said, 'I don't dare believe you.'

'I'm feeling the same way.' She reached out a hand and laid it on his chest, welcoming the solid thunder of his life-force beneath her palm with a relief so intense it made her giddy.

From some final reserve of strength she summoned a smile. 'If you love me, why on earth have you kept away from me ever since we became engaged?'

His hand came up to cover hers and hold it clamped beneath his. She saw belief light his eyes to fire, relax the stark lines of his face, and joy lifted her so high she felt she was flying.

Although Gerd didn't smile, there was a note of humour in his voice when he said, 'Because I'm an idiot! Right at the start, you were so determined to keep our affair without strings that I was sure you couldn't love me.'

'I didn't want you to know I loved you. It seemed so—so *needy*! Especially,' she accused with spirit, 'when you so clearly didn't love me!'

He laughed deeply and began to pull her towards him, his eyes narrowing in the way she'd come to recognise. Her pulse beat heavily, erratically, in her ears.

When they were so close she could feel the warmth of his body, he said, 'But I did—and do—love you. And I want you to be needy where I'm concerned. Because I need you more than the breath in my body, more than anything I have ever coveted.'

'I wish you'd told me,' she said huskily.

His smile was brief and sardonic. 'I wish I'd had the courage,' he admitted. 'Blame it on my pride. I hoped that passion would be enough to break your reliance on Kelt. And that once you had learned to trust me you might learn to love me.'

She shook her head, no longer embarrassed by the bob of her curls around her face. 'Even after seeing me kiss him, I don't know how you could mistake my feelings for Kelt for anything more serious than affection!'

'I was jealous,' he admitted with a wry glance. 'Jealous people don't reason terribly well, and when I'm thinking about you logic and common sense seem to fly out the window. Even when my plan seemed to be working, there was always that stab of jealousy, although I was happy on the island, and you seemed to be too.'

'Oh, yes,' she sighed, colouring. 'Until I got too bold,' she said ruefully.

His swift smile was sexy and reminiscent. 'I liked what you did very much. One day—or night—you'll have to repeat it.' He sobered then, and went on, 'And then I blew it. When I saw the chance to make you mine I couldn't resist. For the first time ever I didn't even care about Carathia; I just used it ruthlessly to persuade you. But you fought the idea with everything you had, and I realised that I'd been fooling myself about your feelings. You truly didn't want to marry me.'

'Oh, no,' she said, her voice trembling. 'I desperately want to marry you. I just didn't want it to be the *sensible* thing to do—a marriage for reasons of state was so cold, so impersonal.'

He gave a snort. 'Impersonal?'

Rosie frowned up at him. 'Well, you made it seem so,' she said forthrightly. 'I wanted to marry you because we loved each other enough to spend the rest of our lives together. It hurt to think it was for convenience.'

'Convenience?' he said incredulously. 'You've thrown my life into disarray, come between me and everything I've been brought up to believe were the most important things in my life, and you call it *convenient*?' He brushed an errant curl back from her face. 'I've never come across a *less* convenient woman. If I could take you to bed right now I'd show you exactly how I feel, but I don't dare do anything—in fact, I shouldn't even be touching you—because in ten minutes or so I'm due to take a call from the Chief Minister about the latest news on the economic fallout, and if I do more than kiss the tip of your nose I won't make it.'

'Far be it from me to keep you away from affairs of state,' she said demurely and stepped back.

'But after that,' he threatened, eyes hot with promise, 'all bets are off.'

Laughing, Rosie watched him go, then hugged herself with incandescent joy. It was too much to take in. After all the pain, the resolution had been so simple, so miraculously inevitable.

She went across to the window and looked out at the mountains. This place would always be precious to her because Gerd had confessed his love for her here.

Somewhere up on those high peaks the white lily bloomed—a link with New Zealand's high country. And on the island in the sunny Adriatic, myrtle bloomed around Aphrodite's temple—another link.

Appropriate that they should be flowers. Her desire for a flower shop seemed a distant, rapidly fading dream now, one she didn't regret. Loving Gerd was enough. And as his wife she'd look for a chance to do something in her favoured field.

She let the drape fall and settled down to write to Hani. If she hadn't loved her before, she thought as she sent the email, she'd love her now for being the—albeit unwitting—cause of this delicious happiness.

Two hours later Gerd came back to a supper table set for two with candles and flowers. He examined the table then said calmly, 'When is this being served?'

'In half an hour,' Rosie said. 'I thought we should drink some champagne first, so I told the butler to find the very best vintage in the cellar.'

Gerd checked the bottle. 'Ah, yes, that's perfect,' he said, and allowed his eyes to linger on her. She was dressed in a silky little shift, her hair pulled back into a ridiculous bobble of curls at the back to reveal the tender, innocent nape of her neck.

He said suddenly, 'Twelve years seemed such a hell of a difference when you were eighteen and I was thirty. It didn't seem so much a couple of hours ago, but right now you look like youth and joy and delight, and that makes me feel old and jaded and rakish.'

'You're none of those things,' she said indignantly. 'Shall we make another promise to each other? Shall we decide never to talk about the difference in ages again? I don't care about it and I don't see why you should.' She laughed up at him, the sunshiny girl he'd fallen in love with so many years before, and said, 'I plan to keep you young, anyway.'

Gerd's doubts fled, leaving him with a deep, intense joy he'd never thought to experience, a feeling of utter rightness. 'I'm more than happy to drink to that,' he said, and popped the cork on the champagne bottle. As he handed her one of the flutes he said, 'I think I must have fallen in love with you when I first kissed you.'

Rosie took a tiny sip. 'If you did, you wasted an awful lot of time before you did anything about it, and even then you had to be seduced into it.'

'*I* seduced *you*,' he said promptly, the hawk eyes gleaming gold. 'As for wasting time—no, I don't think so. You were a child. The years between us put me very definitely in the too-old category. Now they don't matter so much.'

'They don't matter at all,' she said quietly. 'The only thing in the world that does matter is that you love me and I love you. And I will love you forever.'

In the raw, stripped voice of deepest emotion, Gerd said, 'We're well matched, then, because that's exactly how long I plan to love you.'

Later, much later, when they were lying in bed entwined in the delicious, languorous aftermath of passion, Rosie smoothed a hand over his shoulder. 'I'm sorry I bit you. I didn't mean to.'

'Honourable scars,' he said complacently. 'You can bite me any time you want to. Just don't break the skin.'

After she'd kissed the marks better she asked, 'Why have you been so aloof and cold?'

He hugged her closer, and she felt his body tense against her. 'Because I was trying—too late and rather foolishly—to keep what was left of my mind clear during the year it's going to take us to get married.' His chest lifted as he laughed quietly. 'For all the good it did me. And partly to give you room—you were not happy, and I knew I'd forced you into this. I thought you needed time.'

'I needed *you*,' she told him trenchantly. 'Are we going to have to be discreet until we're married?'

'I'm afraid so.'

Rosie shivered as he ran a far from discreet hand over her. 'It's going to be hard,' she said thoughtfully.

'We'll manage.'

She held his hand still. 'When you proposed to me you said I'd be a good wife for you and good for Carathia too. What made you think that?'

After a pause he said, 'I love you, so I knew you'd be a good wife for me. As for Carathia—that's a bit more subtle, but people instinctively like you and enjoy your company. And you're intelligent and beautiful and kind and sensible. What country could ask for more?'

'I hope I can do it,' she said seriously. 'I don't know anything about being a Grand Duchess. I don't want to let you—or the Carathians—down.'

'You won't.' He held her against him, his voice so positive she allowed herself to relax and believe him. 'My grandfather was a New Zealander; he had no idea how to be the husband of the Grand Duchess, but the Carathians adored him. They're more than ready to adore another Kiwi. And you'll have my complete and utter support.'

Rosie said goodbye to the last of her fears. 'So when did you actually decide to marry me?' she asked, wriggling into a more comfortable position against him.

'You're not going to like this,' he said drily.

'Tell me just the same.'

'When I realised you'd been a virgin. It was obviously something you had believed important enough to preserve. Yet you had given it to me.'

Brows wrinkled, Rosie thought about that. 'So your proposal was a—some sort of recompense?'

'I'm getting myself further and further into quicksand,'

he said half-humorously. 'No. I hoped the gift of your virginity meant you felt more for me than casual lust.'

'*Casual?*' she asked on a choked laugh. 'If you thought that was casual…'

He smiled. 'And I suppose I should confess I couldn't bear the thought of anyone else making love to you. The thought of anyone else taking what had been mine filled me with a very uncomfortable possessiveness.' He cupped her chin, tilting her head so that he could see her face. 'You don't seem shocked.'

No, because he was Gerd, Grand Duke of Carathia, and although he lived in the twenty-first century he hadn't entirely shaken off the high-handed attitudes of his ancestors. 'Only a little bit,' she teased.

'And now it's my turn to ask a question. Why were you so convinced I didn't—would never—love you?'

Rosie had rarely revealed her feelings, not even to her friends. She hesitated then looked up at him. This was Gerd, and he loved her.

She said, 'I think it must be that I grew up believing I wasn't lovable. My mother left me, and my father was away so often it sometimes felt as though he'd just abandoned me to the housekeeper. Not that I suffered— Mrs Jameson was always good to me. Alex was away at school for most of the time and the age gap was too big for us to be friends. When I got older, I lived for those holidays at Kiwinui. Kelt became a sort of surrogate brother or father; I felt valued by him.'

Gerd said in a voice that made her cold, 'Apart from Kelt, we were selfish bastards, all of us.'

'No, you weren't,' she objected. 'I was much younger, and a girl—why would any of you want me tagging along? You were all kind; Kelt taught me to swim, you taught me to ride and Alex showed me how to play chess. And your grandmother was lovely. Even my father loved me in his own way, I think.' Her smile was tinged with sadness. 'He just loved other things more.'

Gerd said, 'I should have understood your basic insecurity.'

Heart overflowing, Rosie looked at him. 'How could you? I didn't even understand it myself. My mother's history of affairs gone wrong taught me that passion didn't mean love. But without realising it I must have decided that love was too hard, probably impossible—that I had no right to expect it. So I didn't.'

Gerd lay back on the pillows, his expression sombre. 'I kept thinking—she must know I love her. It has to be so obvious. Kelt knew, Alex knew, Hani knew—how could you not realise it? Yet there was always a barrier, a wall I couldn't breach however often and passionately we made love. And I knew damned well you only wanted an affair.'

She flushed. 'I thought I was being sensible,' she admitted, adding swiftly, 'At least I accepted that it would hurt when it was over!'

Gerd showed his teeth in a smile without humour. 'I suppose it was my damned pride that kept me silent. Two complete idiots,' he said. 'We deserve each other. I knew I was in deep trouble when the prospect of a child gave me an excuse for bulldozing you into agreeing to marry me.'

Rosie's snort was followed by a reluctant admission. 'So while I was angsting over whether or not to marry you and suffering because you didn't love me, you were gloating.'

'Hell, no. I was delighted when you agreed—until I realised exactly what I was doing to you. Because even before we went back to the capital, you started to retreat.'

'*I* retreated?' she exclaimed, startling them both by thumping him in the solar plexus. 'You never came near me—after I said I'd marry you, every night you kissed me on the forehead and left me at my bedroom door. What was I supposed to think?'

He jackknifed up, his face aggressive. Reaching for her, he said grimly, 'I was giving you time to get used to everything—to me as your future husband and Carathia as the place you were going to live—without passion clogging your brain.'

She held herself stiffly away. 'Did it clog yours?'

'Yes,' he said savagely, and kissed her. Then he let her go and got up off the bed, his shoulders set.

Rosie sat up and stared at him. 'I'm glad,' she said abruptly.

Without turning he said, 'It worried the hell out of me because it had never happened before. I told myself I was doing the right thing for Carathia, but I hated it that whenever I looked at you, touched you—hell, even thought of you—it drove any thoughts of duty to my country clear out of my mind.'

'Good.' His words satisfied her last shred of reservation.

He turned to look at her, sleekly golden-ivory in his bed, embedded in his heart. 'It no longer matters,' he said starkly. 'I know now that all I want, all I need, is you.

Carathia will always be important to me, but you—you are at my heart's core, the one, infinitely loved constant in my life.'

Tall and tanned and leanly lithe, he filled her vision. Tears flooded her eyes, and she said in a shaken voice, 'And you are mine. Forever.'

'Forever,' he said like a vow. 'So now, would you like some more of that champagne?'

'No, I'd like something from a much better vintage,' she said sweetly, and laughed, holding out her arms as he tumbled her back onto the bed.

In his eyes she could see love and trust and passion, and she knew that for them this was the first day of their marriage, even though their vows had been informal and for their ears only.

They would have their big wedding to satisfy the good people of Carathia, but from now on they were joined in life and love.

After the wild carnival of bells that had rung her ears for days, Rosie greeted the silence of the villa with relief. Maria had met them at the door, beamed on them both and wished them every happiness, informed them at length of the food she'd left for them, and then departed, leaving them alone.

'Tired?' Gerd asked, slipping his arm around her shoulders.

'A bit,' she acknowledged, then gave a gasping little laugh when he picked her up. 'You won't be able to do this for much longer,' she murmured, gazing up into his face.

'Oh, I think I'll be able to manage three of you for

some months yet,' he said, carefully negotiating the way to the bedroom.

'Twins,' she murmured, still dazed at the news the gynaecologist had given them only three days previously. She looked up at him, her gaze direct. 'We'll be careful of them, won't we? We'll make sure they have the kind of childhood neither of us had—a loving, happy, secure childhood, so they grow up confident and certain of themselves.'

Gerd's arms tightened around her as though she was infinitely precious. 'We will,' he said like a vow. 'I'm seriously thinking of banning all information about the birth so that no one will ever know—apart from you, me and the doctor who delivers them—which one arrives first. That should fool anyone who tries to resurrect that old legend.'

Rosie laughed. 'It should give Carathia breathing time, anyway,' she said. 'But I think your plans for education will do the trick better. By the time any question of the succession comes up—in fifty years from now, say—no one will remember the legend.'

He set her carefully down on the bed and looked at her, slim and glowing, her gold-flecked eyes warm with the love he no longer doubted.

That morning she'd walked towards him in a wedding gown, happiness radiating from her. This time they'd made their vows in public, and Carathia had celebrated the joy and commitment of their Grand Duke and his Duchess with festivities that would outlast the night, but here, in this house, in this room, they were man and woman, two lovers.

Husband and wife.

Gripped by emotion so intense he almost buckled under it, he sat down on the edge of the bed and bent to kiss her throat. Her perfume—soft, all woman—enveloped him, and her arms came around him and hugged him hard.

'How tired are you?' he asked, fighting down a fierce hunger.

Her laugh was slow and sensuous. 'Not too tired,' she whispered into his ear.

Rosie felt his body harden against her and, as they began the slow, deliciously sensual journey towards that passionate place reserved solely for them, she knew that, whatever the future brought, they would face it together. She and Gerd held each other's hearts in safekeeping.

Coming Next Month

from **Harlequin Presents® EXTRA.** Available February 8, 2011.

Coming Next Month

from **Harlequin Presents®.** Available February 22, 2011.

REQUEST YOUR FREE BOOKS!

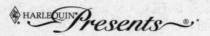

2 FREE NOVELS PLUS
2 FREE GIFTS!

YES! Please send me 2 FREE Harlequin Presents® novels and my 2 FREE gifts (gifts are worth about $10). After receiving them, if I don't wish to receive any more books, I can return the shipping statement marked "cancel." If I don't cancel, I will receive 6 brand-new novels every month and be billed just $4.05 per book in the U.S. or $4.74 per book in Canada. That's a saving of at least 15% off the cover price! It's quite a bargain! Shipping and handling is just 50¢ per book.* I understand that accepting the 2 free books and gifts places me under no obligation to buy anything. I can always return a shipment and cancel at any time. Even if I never buy another book, the two free books and gifts are mine to keep forever.

106/306 HDN E5M4

Name	(PLEASE PRINT)	
Address		Apt. #
City	State/Prov.	Zip/Postal Code

Signature (if under 18, a parent or guardian must sign)

Mail to the **Harlequin Reader Service:**
IN U.S.A.: P.O. Box 1867, Buffalo, NY 14240-1867
IN CANADA: P.O. Box 609, Fort Erie, Ontario L2A 5X3

Not valid for current subscribers to Harlequin Presents books.

**Are you a current subscriber to Harlequin Presents books and want to
receive the larger-print edition? Call 1-800-873-8635 today!**

* Terms and prices subject to change without notice. Prices do not include applicable taxes. N.Y. residents add applicable sales tax. Canadian residents will be charged applicable provincial taxes and GST. Offer not valid in Quebec. This offer is limited to one order per household. All orders subject to approval. Credit or debit balances in a customer's account(s) may be offset by any other outstanding balance owed by or to the customer. Please allow 4 to 6 weeks for delivery. Offer available while quantities last.

Your Privacy: Harlequin Books is committed to protecting your privacy. Our Privacy Policy is available online at www.eHarlequin.com or upon request from the Reader Service. From time to time we make our lists of customers available to reputable third parties who may have a product or service of interest to you. If you would prefer we not share your name and address, please check here. ☐

Help us get it right—We strive for accurate, respectful and relevant communications. To clarify or modify your communication preferences, visit us at www.ReaderService.com/consumerchoice.

HP10R

USA TODAY *bestselling author Lynne Graham*
is back with a thrilling new trilogy
SECRETLY PREGNANT, CONVENIENTLY WED

Three heroines must marry alpha males to keep
their dreams...but Alejandro, Angelo and Cesario
are not about to be tamed!

Book 1—JEMIMA'S SECRET
Available March 2011 from Harlequin Presents®.

JEMIMA yanked open a drawer in the sideboard to find
Alfie's birth certificate. Her son was her husband's child.
It was a question of telling the truth whether she liked it or
not. She extended the certificate to Alejandro.

"This has to be nonsense," Alejandro asserted.

"Well, if you can find some other way of explaining how
I managed to give birth by that date and Alfie not be yours,
I'd like to hear it," Jemima challenged.

Alejandro glanced up, golden eyes bright as blades and
as dangerous. "All this proves is that you must still have
been pregnant when you walked out on our marriage. It
does not automatically follow that the child is mine."

"'I know it doesn't suit you to hear this news now and I
really didn't want to tell you. But I can't lie to you about it.
Someday Alfie may want to look you up and get acquainted."

"If what you have just told me is the truth, if that little
boy does prove to be mine, it was vindictive and extremely
selfish of you to leave me in ignorance!"

Jemima paled. "When I left you, I had no idea that I was
still pregnant."

"Two years is a long period of time, yet you made no
attempt to inform me that I might be a father. I will want
DNA tests to confirm your claim before I make any deci-

sion about what I want to do."

"Do as you like," she told him curtly. "*I* know who Alfie's father is and there has never been any doubt of his identity."

"I will make arrangements for the tests to be carried out and I will see you again when the result is available," Alejandro drawled with lashings of dark Spanish masculine reserve.

"I'll contact a solicitor and start the divorce," Jemima proffered in turn.

Alejandro's eyes narrowed in a piercing scrutiny that made her uncomfortable. "It would be foolish to do anything before we have that DNA result."

"I disagree," Jemima flashed back. "I should have applied for a divorce the minute I left you!"

Alejandro quirked an ebony brow. "And why didn't you?"

Jemima dealt him a fulminating glance but said nothing, merely moving past him to open her front door in a blunt invitation for him to leave.

"I'll be in touch," he delivered on the doorstep.

What is Alejandro's next move? Perhaps rekindling their marriage is the only solution! But will Jemima agree?

Find out in Lynne Graham's
exciting new romance
JEMIMA'S SECRET

Available March 2011
from Harlequin Presents®.

Start your Best Body today with these top 3 nutrition tips!

1. **SHOP THE PERIMETER OF THE GROCERY STORE:** The good stuff—fruits, veggies, lean proteins and dairy—always line the outer edges of the store. When you veer into the center aisles, you enter the temptation zone, where the unhealthy foods live.

2. **WATCH PORTION SIZES:** Most portion sizes in restaurants are nearly twice the size of a true serving and at home, it's easy to "clean your plate." Use these easy serving guidelines:
   - Protein: the palm of your hand
   - Grains or Fruit: a cup of your hand
   - Veggies: the palm of two open hands

3. **USE THE RAINBOW RULE FOR PRODUCE:** Your produce drawers should be filled with every color of fruits and vegetables. The greater the variety, the more vitamins and other nutrients you add to your diet.

Find these and many more helpful tips in

USA TODAY *Bestselling Author*

Lynne Graham

is back with her most exciting trilogy yet!

SECRETLY PREGNANT
CONVENIENTLY WED

Jemima, Flora and Jess aren't looking for love,
but all have babies very much in mind...and they may
just get their wish and more with the wealthiest, most
handsome and impossibly arrogant men in Europe!

Coming March 2011

JEMIMA'S SECRET

Alejandro Navarro Vasquez has long desired vengeance after
his wife, Jemima, betrayed him. When he discovers the
whereabouts of his runaway wife—and that she has a two-
year-old son—Alejandro is determined to settle the score....

FLORA'S DEFIANCE (April 2011)
JESS'S PROMISE (May 2011)

Available exclusively from Harlequin Presents.

HP12975